W9-COV-183

The Bear Makers

The Bear Makers

ANDREA CHENG

FRONT STREET
Asheville, North Carolina

ALSO BY ANDREA CHENG
Marika
Honeysuckle House
The Lace Dowry
Eclipse
Tire Mountain
Where the Steps Were

To Oma and Grams, the bear makers
—A.C.

Text copyright © 2008 by Andrea Cheng
Photographs copyright © 2008 by Jane Cheng
All rights reserved
Printed in the United States of America
Designed by Helen Robinson
First edition

LIBRARY OF CONGRESS CATALOGING-IN-PUBLICATION DATA
Cheng, Andrea.
The bear makers / Andrea Cheng.—1st ed.
p. cm.
Summary: In post-World War II Budapest, a young girl and her
family struggle against the oppressive Hungarian
Worker's Party policies and try to find a way to a better life.
ISBN 978-1-59078-518-8 (hardcover : alk. paper)
1. Hungary—History—1945–1989—Juvenile fiction.
[1. Hungary—History—1945–1989—Fiction.
2. Family life—Hungary—Fiction.] I. Title.
PZ7.C41943Be 2008
[Fic]—dc22
2007049005

FRONT STREET
An Imprint of Boyds Mills Press, Inc.
815 Church Street
Honesdale, Pennsylvania 18431

The Bear Makers

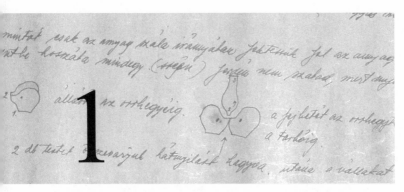

1

"Mama," I ask my mother, "when will you be finished?"

Mama stops pushing the treadle of the sewing machine and looks up. "What is it you need, Kata?"

"Nothing. I just want to know when you'll be done."

Mama sighs. "Not for a long time. Not until you are asleep."

"Are you making another bear?"

"Yes, Kata."

"What should we name this one?"

"It's better if we don't name him. That way you won't be sad when he leaves."

"I like the name Miklos. If I have a boy someday, that's what I'll name him."

"Okay, Kata. Now go to sleep."

"Mama?"

"What is it?"

"When is Bela coming home?"

"When the study session is over, he will come."

"What about Papa?"

"He is with your brother. Now, please, Kata, go to sleep."

"Why do they always have to go to study sessions?"

"If they don't, they may get into trouble."

"What kind of trouble?"

"That is hard to know, Kata. These days everyone is watching everyone else."

"Watching for what?"

"It's better if Papa and Bela just go to the study sessions."

Mama is moving the treadle slowly. She must be making the bear's ear. "Mama, is that the bear's ear?"

She doesn't answer.

I raise my voice. "Mama, will the bear be ready in the morning?"

"If you don't go to sleep, I won't be able to finish."

"Who is this one for?"

"Auntie Klari may buy him for her grandson Imre, who is sick."

"Can I play with him first?"

"Eleven years old, and you still want to play with a stuffed bear?" Mama sighs. "Okay. You can play with him if your hands are clean."

The sewing machine makes a *click-click* noise when the needle goes through the fabric. Much later, our apartment door opens and I hear the low voice of my brother Bela whispering with Mama in the dark. They are having a cup of tea. Mama says, "Be patient, Bela."

Bela's voice is loud. "I have waited too long already. All through the war, I waited. After it was all over, I had hope. We even had free elections. But by now—"

"Shh, Bela, Kata is sleeping."

Bela lowers his voice so I can barely hear. "Last week the Secret Police called two of my classmates in for questioning."

Mama sucks in her breath. "What did the AVO want with them?"

"Want? What do they ever want?" My brother is raising his voice again. "They want us to inform on our friends, our relatives, our parents."

"Shh, Bela. Tell me what happened to your classmates."

"For three hours they were questioned."

"What were they asked?"

"What do you do for the people? How do you contribute to the success of the Hungarian Workers' Party? Why were you seen talking to so-and-so last week? If you don't want trouble, come back next week with five names for us."

My mother puts down her cup. "Okay, they were questioned and released. Nothing happened."

"Next time they might not be so lucky. Mama, you don't understand. We are being watched."

"Who would be watching us, I ask you?"

"Our neighbors, our friends, anyone."

"Shh, Bela, everything is okay."

"Mama, can't you see? The situation is going from bad to worse. Next time the AVO could call me in. And I might not be as lucky as my classmates."

"Be patient, Bela. It takes time to rebuild the country. And there are always setbacks along the way."

"Do you call arresting people and forcing them to inform on their parents a setback? Mama, I cannot wait here in Budapest forever."

I sit up. There is a soft, wet sound. Is that Mama crying? Teacups clink on the counter. Bela goes into his room and shuts the door. Why would anyone be watching us? Why does Bela say he has been waiting too long? Waiting for what?

I am the one who is always waiting, not Bela. Every day I wait for school to be out. I wait for Bela to come home. I wait for Eva to play with me. I wait for Mama to finish the bears.

I tiptoe to Bela's room, which is really just a storage closet, and open the door a crack. My brother is a mound underneath a blue blanket. "Bela?" I whisper. I want to curl up with him, but he is already asleep.

2

The room is full of light. How could I have slept so long? On a chair next to my bed is a perfect bear. His fur is soft and golden. His glass eyes catch the morning sun. I sit him on my stomach.

"Kata, come and have breakfast," Mama calls.

I take the bear with me into the kitchen. "Where is Papa?"

"He and Bela are hiking today."

"Why didn't they take me?"

"Because it is a hiking study group."

The hot cereal is warm and sweet. I hold a spoon close to Miklos Bear's mouth so he can have a taste.

"Kata, don't do that. The bear will get dirty and then how will I sell him to Auntie Klari?"

"I'm not touching his mouth with the spoon."

"But some can drip onto the fur. Kata, you are acting like a baby."

Mama tells me that all the time, but I don't see what's so babyish about playing with a bear. I bet Eva would play with a bear too if she had one.

A drop of cereal falls onto the bear's leg. Mama snatches him off the table. "You are not listening."

I look down at my bowl. I am done eating breakfast.

Eva's apartment is right below mine. I knock on the door and wait. It takes Eva a long time to open the door. We used to play school, and she was the teacher and I was the naughty pupil who got into trouble. Then we started playing beauty shop. I am the hairdresser because I can braid hair better than she can, even though she's two years older. Auntie Erzsi taught me how to make the braids tight and even. But now that Eva's thirteen, sometimes she doesn't want to play anything.

"Hey, Kata." She squeezes out into the hallway. "I have something to show you."

We go around back into the small garden and sit on the wall with the sun warming our backs.

Eva takes a red scarf out of her pocket. "A Pioneer scarf," she says.

"It looks just like my scarf, only mine is blue."

Eva swirls it in the air. "It's not at all the same, Kata." She takes a deep breath. "Because this red scarf is part of the Hungarian flag."

"Did they cut up the flag?"

Eva sighs. "You're too young to understand. It's a *symbol* of the flag, not the real flag." She puts the red scarf around her neck and ties it into a knot in front. "You wear it like this, and then you are a Young Pioneer."

"What do Young Pioneers do?"

Eva pulls her eyebrows together and stands up straight. "We work hard to help the people."

"How?"

She jumps off the wall and stands at attention. "Like this," she says, marching in place.

We take turns wearing the red scarf and marching around the edge of the garden. Eva keeps repeating, "Work is honor and glory." She tells me to repeat it after her, so I do. Then she takes off the scarf and waves it in front of my face.

"Do you want to play beauty shop now?" I ask. Playing Young Pioneer is making me tired.

Eva pulls her eyebrows together. "Kata, don't you see, this is very important. This is not a game."

Bela and my father are walking up the hill. Bela is ahead, taking big steps. Papa is bent over like an old man.

"Your father looks like a grandfather," Eva says.

I hop off the wall. "I'd better go eat lunch," I say.

"Okay, Comrade," Eva says, tying the scarf around her neck and standing at attention.

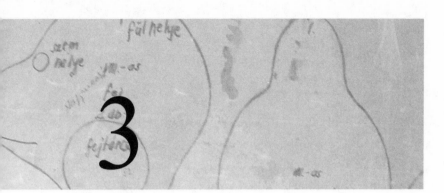

3

I want Bela to play the mill game with me like he used to, but he says he is busy.

"Please."

He shakes his head. "Sorry."

"You are always busy," I say, folding my arms across my chest. "And I don't think you are really sorry."

Papa is setting up the chessboard. He and his friend Uncle Sandor play on Sunday afternoons.

Bela puts on his hat. "Where are you going?" I ask him.

"To meet Andras and Jancsi."

"Can I go with you?"

"Not today."

"You always say that."

"We have important issues to discuss."

"Stop bothering your brother," Mama says to me, adjusting Bela's hat. "Now, don't be home too late," she tells him. She stands on her tiptoes to give Bela a kiss. He goes down the stairs and out the door of our building.

From the balcony I watch my brother cross the street and head downhill to meet his friends. He is stooped over just a little, like Papa. I wish I could run after him and grab his hand. We could stop at the park. When I was little, Bela used to push me on the swings, higher than all the other kids, so high that I was above the rooftops.

Bela stops at the corner and waves. Even if he can't see me, he knows I am watching. I wave back with my white handkerchief.

The October wind is blowing and I am shivering, but I can't take my eyes off my brother. I won't go back inside until he comes home again. I will just stand here and wait.

A NEW NAME   *September 1944, Visegrád*

Bela is always inside the farmhouse. He reads the The Count of Monte Cristo *over and over because he doesn't have any other books. I want him to come and see Softy the goat and the kitten who still doesn't have a name, but he won't. There is a war, Kata, he whispers. Don't you see?*

But the war is only in Budapest. We took the train to Visegrád and then walked up a big hill to Auntie Erzsi's farm, where Bela and I will stay until the war is over. On the farm I have a new name. I am not Steiner Kata anymore. Mama says Steiner is a Jewish name and now I am Voros Kata. It is very important never to say my old name. We don't want anyone to know we are Jewish and we cannot cause Auntie Erzsi any trouble. We have to help her on the farm. Bela doesn't like animals, but I do, so I help Auntie Erzsi feed the chickens and the hogs. I pet the kitten and give him milk. I promise Mama that I

15

will not cause trouble and I will not wander off. She will come back to visit whenever she can. She can't stay with Auntie Erzsi because it would be too crowded. Papa is working somewhere far away, so he might not be able to visit for a while.

Bela will take care of you on the farm, Mama says. Listen to your big brother.

Never say your old name. Bela has his face so close to mine that I can see tiny hairs above his lip that were not there before. Do you understand, Kata?

Mama already told me that. Voros Kata, Voros Bela, Voros Matyas, and Voros Etus. Bela, will you come with me to see the baby goat now? Please?

Kata, you are a pest.

I go by myself and Softy is waiting for me. That goat follows me all around wherever I go, just like a dog. Bela comes outside and says, See, Kata, you don't listen. You are wandering again.

"Kata, it's cold on the balcony. Come and get your jacket. We are going shopping."

I want to stay home. The lines everywhere are long, and standing makes my legs tired and my back ache. "Do I have to go?"

"You can help me carry the bags."

We see a line outside of the butcher shop, so we stand there first. Mama asks the lady ahead of us, "What are we waiting for here?"

The lady shrugs. "I hear they have something special."

Eva and her mother are just coming out of the shop with a big package wrapped in brown paper. "Hi, Kata," Eva says, turning so I can see her red scarf.

"Nice veal chops they have," Eva's mother says.

Mama nods.

"See you later." Eva takes her mother's arm.

By the time we get to the front of the line, an hour has gone by. My legs are tired and the butcher has nothing but a few fatty slices of bacon.

"I'd like veal chops," my mother says.

"They are all gone," the butcher says.

"What do you have, then?"

He points to the fatty bacon. "You can see it right here."

"No thank you," Mama says, pulling me along.

"Why does Eva's mother always get veal chops?" I ask, disappointed.

"They have connections," Mama whispers. "Now hurry. We have one more stop to make." We head across Lenin Street to the fabric store.

The lady there knows my mother. "Etus," she says, putting her hand on my mother's arm, "I've been saving something just for you." She reaches under the counter and takes out a big roll of yellow plastic. "This is very modern," she says, showing Mama a purse she has sewn out of it.

Mama turns the purse around in her hands, inspecting the lining and working the zipper. "Very nice," she says. "How much is a meter?"

"Twenty forints."

Mama gasps. "Twenty forints?"

"It comes from the West," the lady whispers. "They use it in Vienna, Paris, London."

"But in Paris they earn more money," Mama says.

"We all have to make ends meet," the lady says, starting to put the plastic back underneath the counter.

Mama is looking at the purse again. "Okay," she says. "I'll take three meters."

We watch the lady measure the plastic and cut it carefully on the line. "I gave you a few extra centimeters," she says, folding it into a neat square.

Mama gives her the money and hands me the package. "Come, Kata, it's time to go home."

The sidewalk is full of hurrying people. The wind has picked up and it is drizzling. I shiver through my jacket.

"Why did you buy that ugly plastic?" I ask Mama.

"It's an investment," Mama answers.

"What's an investment?"

"Shh. It is a way to earn money."

"I thought Papa earned the money."

"Not enough, Kata. His salary has been reduced. That is why I am selling the bears."

"And handbags too?"

"I sell whatever people will buy," Mama says. "But remember, Kata. Don't tell anybody. Our money is nobody's business."

We are hurrying up the hill because the rain is coming down hard. We turn in to our apartment and I can smell Eva's veal chops. "What are we having for lunch?" I ask.

"Cabbage and potatoes," Mama says.

"Eva is lucky," I say, sniffing deeply.

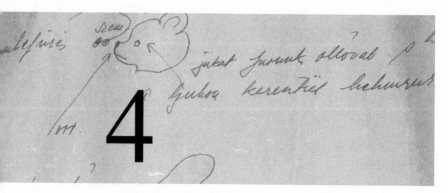

4

For many days, Mama works on handbag patterns. One is too wide, the next too tall. "It doesn't have to be perfect," I say.

"Nobody wants to buy a handbag where you have to dig to find your belongings," Mama says, trimming a little off the top.

"Can we go to the park?" I ask Mama.

"Not now, Kata. I have to finish the handbag. Anyway, it's too cold outside."

"Can I go by myself, then?"

"Kata, please. Be patient."

"Most children my age are allowed to go places alone."

Mama isn't listening. Papa and Uncle Sandor are setting up the chessboard. Uncle Sandor smiles at me. "Kata, you grow an inch each week. Come closer so I can measure."

I stand next to his chair and he hugs me with the cigar smell that I like. "Look, Kata, here's a bug," he says, pointing to the collar of my shirt.

I know there's no bug, but I look anyway. Uncle Sandor laughs and touches my cheek. "Still a little girl, your Kata," he says to Papa.

"For a short while," Papa says.

I sit on the sofa with Miklos Bear and watch Papa and Uncle Sandor move the chess pieces on the board. Sometimes one of them says, *Check.* It's such a long and boring game. Papa tried to explain it to me once, but I couldn't keep track of which pieces were allowed to move where.

I could go see if Eva wants to play. But I don't really like playing Young Pioneer. And yesterday when I stopped, Eva said, "I'm busy." She didn't say, *How about tomorrow?* She didn't flip my braid or take my arm.

I haven't seen Bela for a whole week. When I leave for school, he is already at the university, and when I get home, he is out with his friends, Andras, Jancsi, Laszlo, Gyuri. I've heard their names, but I don't even know who they are. Then there's Julia and Anna and Marta. On the farm he was always there on the bed with his book unless he went to the outhouse. But now I can't find my brother.

OUTHOUSE   *October 1944, Visegrád*

Bela wakes me up when it's still dark. Kata, wake up. Come with me and guard the outhouse.

Not now, Bela. Nobody will bother you in the middle of the night.

Kata, come on. Now. Bela pulls me out of bed. He says, Kata, you don't understand, the neighbor boys want to catch me with my pants down. Then they will know I am Jewish, and they will kill us.

How will they know? Your name is Voros Bela.

There are other ways to know besides a name, Kata.

You are crazy. They want you to play soccer because they are short one player, that's what they want. They want to know why you never come outside. They want to know what's wrong with you that you never go past the edge of the yard. They never said one thing about your pants.

Kata, come on. I have to pee. You stand outside the door, and if somebody comes, yell, yell loud, and I'll climb over the back, okay?

I stand outside the door with my arms crossed. I am a good goalkeeper. I won't let anyone through. Then we hurry back into the house as fast as we can.

"Checkmate."

That means the chess game is over. Papa has lost. They put all of the chess pieces into the wooden box until next week.

Then Uncle Sandor says to Papa, "What's going on, Matyas? You cannot concentrate these days."

Papa looks down. "Things do not look good," he says.

"They will improve," Uncle Sandor says. When he smiles, he has many lines around his eyes.

"I am waiting," Papa says.

"Aren't we all," Uncle Sandor says.

Papa shakes his head. "I always seem to be on the wrong side of things."

Uncle Sandor pats Papa on the back. "Don't talk like that, Matyas."

Papa shrugs. "It's true, isn't it? First they took my factory because I was a Jew. Then they gave it back and let me build it up again. When they saw how well it was going, they said it belonged to the state."

"Look at it this way. At least you have a job. And you have a wonderful little girl." He winks at me.

Papa shakes his head. "I hear that lately they are calling people in for 'questioning.'"

"But why would they call you?" Uncle Sandor says. "A simple factory worker?"

"All it takes is for someone to say that I have shown capitalist tendencies." Papa is whispering.

"Look, Matyas—why would anybody say that? Things will improve soon. You'll see."

"You are the eternal optimist," Papa says, sighing.

"And you are the eternal pessimist," Uncle Sandor says. He opens the door. "See you next week, if not before." He winks at me. "And next week, your papa will be the winner."

Papa lies down on the sofa. "What does 'eternal' mean?" I ask him.

"Forever."

"And what is an optimist?"

Papa has his eyes closed. He turns toward the wall. If Bela were home, I could ask him and he would tell me a big long story to explain the word. But where is my brother?

I go downstairs and look for Eva, but nobody is home.

Then I hear voices from behind the garden wall. There she is, huddled with a tall girl I've never seen before. They are whispering and giggling. I crouch behind the wall, trying to hear their muffled words. The girl is talking about someone named Pali. "Did he kiss you on the lips?" Eva asks. "Of course on the lips," the girl says. "What about you?" The girls are moving away from the wall toward the gate. Arm in arm, they leave the garden.

I run back up to my apartment and sit on the floor with Miklos Bear. Who cares if Eva has a new friend? I have a new golden bear. Auntie Klari has still not come for him. What I really wish is that I had a baby goat or a kitten. I wish I were still on the farm with Auntie Erzsi and the animals.

The first time we went back to visit we took Auntie Erzsi a beautiful linen tablecloth with matching napkins that she liked very much. But we could stay only a little while because we had to catch the train. There was no time to see the animals.

SUGAR *October 1944, Visegrád*

Bela says sugar is very precious. It's not for a goat, but I put some in my pocket anyway and the baby goat licks it from my hand. After that, the baby goat dies. He is lying on his side on the ground. The neighbor boys, Peter and Gabor, say baby goats die all the time, but I cannot stop crying. When I tell Bela, he says it is just a goat. I say, I gave it sugar and then it died, and he says, Don't be silly.

Sugar never killed anything. He says, Don't worry about it when animals die. They are only animals, not people. We have to worry only about people like Mama and Papa and Papa's sister and our little cousin Aranka and Grandma and Grandpa. I say, We don't have to worry about people because they can take care of themselves, but animals can't. Auntie Erzsi says, Bela, don't scare your little sister.

I can toss Miklos Bear any way I want and he won't ever die because he's just a stuffed animal.

"Kata, be gentle with the bear," Mama says. "Auntie Klari is coming soon."

I make the bear dance even more. If his arms come loose, Auntie Klari will decide not to buy him.

Mama is at the sewing machine again. She is quilting the plastic with some white stuffing between two layers. She uses that for the sides of the handbag to make them stiff. She holds it up and snips a little sliver off the top. Then she makes an oval-shaped bottom and sews a zipper into the top. It would be a nice bag except for the color.

I hold Miklos Bear by the arms and toss him as high as I can. He lands face down on the floor.

"Kata, what did I just tell you?"

I don't answer.

Mama picks Miklos Bear up and puts him next to her on the sewing machine. She moves the treadle and the needle goes up and down. I fold my arms across my chest and kick at the rug with my foot. The front door opens. I run to my brother and bury my face in his jacket. It smells like leaves and cigarettes.

"Where were you for so long?" Mama asks.

"Sorry," he says, patting my head. "We forgot about the time."

Sorry. Bela always says sorry when he's not sorry at all. If he were really sorry, he wouldn't leave me alone all the time with no friends and nothing to do but watch Mama sew and Papa sleep on the sofa. Then I am sobbing.

Papa sits up. "What's going on?" he asks, putting on his glasses.

Bela is stroking my head with his cold hands.

"Kata is a spoiled little girl," Mama says.

"That I know." My brother's voice is teasing. "But it is not a reason to cry."

"She doesn't listen to me," Mama says. Her voice is sharp. She is sewing again.

"What's wrong?" Bela asks me.

"Miklos Bear," I mumble.

Bela picks up the bear. "Here. Let me dust him off," he says. "Now look, he's perfect."

I shrug. "So what. He's not even mine."

The doorbell rings and there is Eva. "Hey, Kata, I wonder if you want to come with me to the meeting."

"Meeting?"

"The Young Pioneers. Remember?" She shows me her red scarf.

I look at Mama. "May I?"

My mother looks at Bela.

"I think Kata is too young to be a Pioneer," Bela says to Eva. "Aren't you supposed to be in middle school to wear the red scarf?"

"Our leader said we should bring a friend," Eva says. Her face is flushed. She really wants me to come with her.

"Even a younger friend?"

Eva nods. "She said it would be good to introduce new children to our group."

"Anyway, next year I'll be in middle school too," I say, standing up so straight that I am almost as tall as Eva.

Mama's eyes meet mine. I know what she is thinking. *Almost in middle school but acting like a six-year-old.* Mama sighs. "All right. Go wash your face so you don't look as if your mother just beat you. And then you can go."

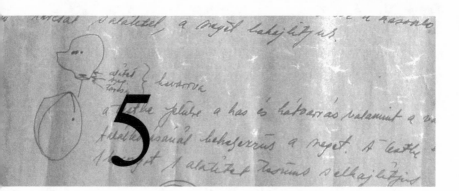

We walk along Mayakovsky Street to the streetcar stop. When we get on, Eva takes my hand and we sit next to each other. A fat lady sits on the edge of our seat, so we have to squish together. I smile because Eva's braid is tickling me. We both have hair that sticks out the sides of our braids, only mine is black and curly and hers is brown and straight. Eva looks at me and then sideways at the fat lady.

"What will we do at the meeting?" I ask.

"Discuss important things."

"Is it like the Little Drummers at my school?"

"It's much more serious than that, Kata. The Little Drummers is for babies."

"Will we sing songs?"

"Yes, lots of songs."

"What songs do you sing?"

"The Young Pioneers' March is one."

"I don't know that. Can you teach it to me?"

The tune is familiar, but I have trouble remembering the words. They are something about a boy who dies for honor and glory.

"I like the song about the bells ringing. Do you know it?" I ask Eva, starting to hum the familiar tune.

"We don't sing old-fashioned songs like that," she says, pulling me off the streetcar at the next stop.

The meeting is in the basement of Eva's school. Everyone sits in a circle and Eva introduces me as Little Comrade Steiner Kata. She tells the leader, Comrade Toth, that I will be officially joining the Young Pioneers next year when I am in middle school. Comrade Toth smiles and says, "Welcome, Kata." Then she thanks Eva for bringing a new member into our group. Eva sits up very straight. We sing the song that Eva taught me on the streetcar. After a few verses I catch on, and my voice is clear and strong. My teacher always says I'm the best singer in my class.

We make red, white, and green flags with a red star in the middle out of paper. Comrade Toth comes over and says my Hungarian flag is perfect. I'm good at cutting. Mama is always saying I learned to use scissors before I could hold a pencil. I glue my flag perfectly onto the stick. There's extra red paper, so I make a red balloon that looks like it is full of air. Last year my uncle gave me a red balloon on my birthday. I find a piece of thread on the floor and glue it to the balloon.

"I like that," says the girl next to me. "It looks so real."

Comrade Toth comes over. "That is a nice balloon, Kata, but we are making flags, not balloons." She picks up my balloon and takes it to her desk.

Blood rushes to my face. I should have made only a flag, like everyone else. Comrade Toth is frowning. Eva pokes me in the side and shows me her flag, which is a little bit crooked. I make two more perfect flags that look like they are actually waving in the breeze. I want Comrade Toth to see, but she's not looking my way.

It's time to plan activities for the coming months. My stomach is growling. I should have had a bigger breakfast and I want to go home. I wonder if Eva still has leftover veal chops. Mama has been cooking meat on Sundays, so today there will be some. I wish we could have meat every day like we used to. I also wish Auntie Mari were still working for us, because she made the best stuffed peppers in the world. Mama says maybe someday Auntie Mari can work for us again, but for now you are not allowed to hire people to cook and clean, and anyway it would be too expensive.

Eva pokes me. "Pay attention," she whispers.

When the weather warms up, we are going to go on a hike, Comrade Toth says. It is important to be strong and fit. We will hike up the hill for a picnic. Everyone is to bring a snack. We should wear comfortable shoes and a jacket in case it rains.

We recite a poem and then the meeting is adjourned. Comrade Toth hands me a red scarf.

"I am not a real Pioneer yet," I say.

"Soon enough," she says, tying the scarf around my neck. She smiles at me and pats my head so I know she isn't mad anymore. She tells Eva, "Thank you for bringing your young friend. She has a beautiful voice." Then to me she says, "Maybe someday you can come with me to a grown-up meeting and sing a song for all the people. Would you like to do that?"

"Yes, thank you," I say, smiling.

I wonder what Comrade Toth will do with my red balloon. It is still there on the desk. I'd like to take it home and give it to Bela, but I'm afraid to ask her to give it back. Maybe she wants to put my red balloon up on the wall of her room.

On the way back on the streetcar, Eva is very quiet. She is almost asleep, so I watch out the window to make sure we don't miss our stop. I see my reflection in the glass. The red scarf looks good on my white sweater. I look older, as if I could be in middle school already. I sit up straight in the seat and smile at the passengers around me. There is a lady with her little son. He is looking at my scarf.

When we get to our stop, Eva is so sleepy she stumbles off the streetcar. I take her arm and we walk slowly up the hill to our building. "Thank you," I say, "for taking me."

"You're welcome," she says. "I'll come get you for the next meeting."

For a minute I'm not sure I want to go again. I like the singing and the crafts, but the meeting is so long and I get so hungry and Comrade Toth took my picture away. Eva says again, "I'll come get you, okay?"

I like the red scarf. If I don't go, I can't wear it. "Okay."

"Say 'Okay, Comrade.'"

"Okay, Comrade."

31

6

Auntie Klari is talking to Mama. She is looking at the handbag and a small comb holder that Mama made to match. Miklos Bear is still sitting on the sewing machine table.

"This is very special," Auntie Klari says. Then with her voice low she continues, "You know, Etus, I have so many friends who would love to have such a handbag with matching accessories. Have you seen those ugly black handbags in all the stores? People are dying for something new and colorful. I'll take the orders and you make the bags. There will be so many orders that you will hardly be able to keep up. Then I'll take a few forints for my trouble and you keep the rest."

Mama nods. "Look at this." She shows Auntie Klari a cosmetics case.

"I love it," Auntie Klari says. She takes out a big stack of bills. "Here, this is for the handbag with the comb holder and the cosmetics case."

I hold my breath.

"And for the bear." She picks up Miklos Bear and holds

him against her stomach. "Imre will love him. And you know how sick that poor boy has been these days."

Mama nods. "I hope he'll feel better soon. When spring comes, the sun will give him strength."

"We can only hope." Auntie Klari looks down. "Spring will be a while yet." She sighs. "Well, I'd better get going. And I'll let you know about the orders." She pats the handbag.

"Yes," Mama says, walking her to the door of our apartment. "And thank you."

"Where's Bela?" I ask as soon as Auntie Klari is gone.

"Out," my mother answers.

I lie down on my bed. "When can we go to visit Auntie Erzsi again?"

"I don't know, Kata. You can see that I have a lot of work to do."

"I wish you didn't have to make all those handbags. Can we take one to Auntie Erzsi when we go?"

Mama sighs. "That's a good idea. When I have time to take you."

"When will I be old enough to go to Visegrád by myself?"

"Not for a while, Kata." Mama sits down at the sewing machine.

My brother is out and Miklos Bear is gone and my mother will not stop sewing and I can't go to visit Auntie Erzsi and I am hungry and the red scarf around my neck is hot and scratchy. I take it off and weave it between my fingers. It's just a red piece of material. Mama and I could make scarves like this in a minute. Miklos Bear is gone. He's not dead, but if I can't see him anymore, what difference does it make? Still, a stuffed bear is never alive, so it cannot die.

LOOKING FOR SOFTY   *October 1944, Visegrád*

Peter and Gabor throw the dead baby goat into the woods. I go to look for it, but I can't find it anywhere. Bela comes running after me and says he'll spank me if I wander off again. I say I'm not wandering, I'm looking for Softy, the baby goat, so I can bury him. Bela drags me back and says he won't let me go out by myself anymore. Auntie Erzsi says, Don't be so strict, Bela. She holds me and says she wishes she had a daughter like me because boys are different. She brushes my hair and braids it and puts the braid around my head like a crown. Can you teach me how to do that, Auntie Erzsi? I practice on her hair, longer than mine but not so thick. Then we both have crowns like the Queen and the Princess.

When we are in bed, Bela makes a mill game out of paper and plays with me. I win twice and he wins once, so I am the champion. I think maybe he let me win on purpose. Then Bela says he would never really spank me. I already knew that.

Mama has made stuffed peppers! I can hardly believe it. They are not as sweet as Auntie Mari's, but still they are very good, and I eat so many that I think I will burst. Mama smiles. "I don't know where you put all the food you eat," she says.

"In here," I say, patting my full stomach.

7

After dinner, Papa makes the sofa into a bed and spreads out the blankets. He is going to sleep.

"Why so early?" I ask.

"Because I have to report to the office an hour earlier now."

"Why?"

"So the new boss can read the newspaper to us." Papa shakes his head.

"Why can't you read the newspaper yourself?"

"I was wondering the same thing," Papa says.

Mama looks sternly at Papa. "Does it hurt you to listen?"

"The guy hardly went to school. He reads very poorly."

"Not everyone can be such a brain."

"There is nothing worth reading in that newspaper."

Mama puts her finger to her lips. "Shh, Papa. Don't say things like that. Kata, now go and get ready for bed. I have work to do."

"Why can't Papa read the newspaper himself?" I ask Mama.

"Because they think we are idiots," Papa says, ignoring Mama's request to be quiet. He raises his voice. "As if there were a thing to believe in that newspaper anyway." He shakes his head. "This morning my boss read that the production of goods in the Soviet Union and its allies has more than doubled in the last six months. Then why is it that there is not enough to buy in the stores? And what there is, is of such poor quality that nobody wants it anyway."

"Papa," Mama says sharply. "Do you want more trouble than we already have?"

I go to my room to change into my pajamas. Mama comes in to say good night. "When's Bela coming home?" I ask.

"After his meeting."

"When is that?"

"I don't know. Kata, don't say anything to anyone about what Papa said. The newspaper just prints the news."

I nod.

"And don't say anything about the bears and the handbags."

"Why not?"

"Because, as I told you, it's nobody's business."

"Can I tell Eva?"

"No, don't tell Eva either." Mama stands up.

"Mama?"

"What is it?"

"Will you make a bear for me?"

"One day I will."

•

I can't fall asleep. The quilt is too hot, but when I take it off, I shiver. If Bela were home, he would come to my room and tell me a story about when I was a baby before the war. He would tell me about how I crawled all over the apartment and got into his things. One day he decided he'd had enough, so he taped my hands to the floor. Mama was so mad. She told him he was a bad big brother, but really he is the best brother in the world.

ORPHANS   *December 1944, Visegrád*

Peter asks if me and Bela are orphans and if that's why we are staying with our aunt.

I say no, it's just that our parents are too busy to take care of us, but they'll come soon and take us back to Budapest.

That's weird, Peter says. Even busy parents take care of their children. Except Jews.

They kill babies and eat them, Gabor says. They drink their blood.

That's at Easter, not at Christmas, Peter says.

Gabor kicks the ball and it rolls crooked. For Christmas I'm getting a new soccer ball. What are you getting, Kata?

I don't know. I'd better go now. I have to help my aunt cook dinner. My legs are like jelly so I can hardly walk.

Bela holds me on his lap. What's wrong, Kata? Don't worry, those boys are just talking nonsense.

•

The wind is blowing and sleet is hitting the windowpanes.
It's past two in the morning and I can still hear the sound of
the sewing machine needle going up and down. It makes a
tak tak sound when the needle goes through the plastic, so I
know Mama is making a handbag, not a bear. I tiptoe over
to Bela's room and open the door. His bed is still empty.
I hear Papa's deep voice over the clicking of the sewing
machine.

"My pay has been cut again."

"Just yours?"

"A few of us were called in." He lowers his voice. "None
of us are members of the Hungarian Workers' Party."

"I see."

"And for that, I have to get up at five in the morning
in this freezing weather and listen to somebody read me a
newspaper that contains not a single word of truth."

"Shhh. Kata is asleep."

"After all that we have been through, now this?" Papa
is shouting.

"Shh, Papa. It won't be so bad. You'll see."

"That's what we said in 1943. Wait it out. If this is the
worst it gets, we can manage. But then—" Papa's voice
cracks.

"Shh, Papa, those times are past. Now nobody is being
killed." Mama's voice is smooth and soft. "This is just temporary, Papa. You'll see."

I tiptoe over to the door. Mama is patting Papa's back.

She says that when things change, there is turmoil for a little while, but then things settle down. She tells him to be patient. Nobody is dying. Papa has his head down on the sewing table. Mama is patting his hair.

"Shh, Papa, you will see. We have to be patient." Mama rubs his shoulders. "Shhh. Kata is asleep. We must be quiet."

"I'm not asleep," I say, pushing open the door of my room. I run to my father and bury my face in his sweater. Then I am crying because of the baby goat that died and because we are tired of always waiting for everything.

8

When I get home from school, Auntie Klari and Mama
are talking in low voices. Auntie Klari has a whole list of
people who want yellow plastic handbags with matching
cases for a comb and cosmetics. She and Mama are trying
to decide on a price.

"If they are too expensive, nobody will buy them,"
Mama says.

"Not true, Etus. People don't have much money, but they
are willing to spend on something that is both high quality
and beautiful. These days they are tired of the same hats,
the same shoes, the same everything." Auntie Klari picks
up the cosmetics case and turns it around in her hands. "The
design is so fashionable, like something you could find in
a department store in Paris." Auntie Klari smiles. "Do you
remember, Etus, the small shop on Vaci Street? They used
to sell quality bags like this."

Mama nods.

"I think we should charge at least eight forints for the
bag and two more for each accessory."

Mama sucks in her breath. "Eight forints? You could

buy a week's worth of groceries for that much money."

Auntie Klari puts her hand on Mama's. "Your work is worth a lot of groceries." Then she lowers her voice even more. "How about asking a couple of people to help you out? Of course, you are the designer, but they can do some of the sewing for you."

"You are quite the business lady, Klari," Mama says. She goes over to the radio and turns the volume up so nobody else can hear what she is saying. "But this worries me a bit."

Auntie Klari looks sideways at my mother. "Who has to know? You like to sew. You make gifts for your friends. Is that a problem?"

"But word could get out." Mama is whispering now. The radio is playing some kind of march. "You know, neighbors are always watching."

Auntie Klari winks at my mother. "Think about it, Etus. We'll talk again. Oh, I forgot to tell you how much Imre adores the bear. He drags him around everywhere. You know what he has named him? Bruno. Bruni, he calls him. His cousin would like a bear too. Now I'd better get going."

"Thank you, Klari," Mama says. "You are a big help to us."

"And you to us," Auntie Klari says.

"Does Imre's cousin want a golden bear?" I ask.

"Any color will be fine," Auntie Klari answers.

"What will he name the bear?" I ask.

Auntie Klari looks at me with her eyebrows together. "I have no idea, Kata." She shuts the door of our apartment softly, and I can hear her high heels on the steps.

•

While I do my homework, Mama takes a big piece of paper and draws the pattern pieces for a handbag, a comb holder, and a cosmetics case.

"Mama?"

"Yes, Kata."

"Bruno is a dumb name for a bear."

Mama is erasing the lines she has drawn and redrawing them. "Kata, the name doesn't make any difference. Now do your homework."

All afternoon Mama struggles with the pattern pieces. She has decided to make the bottom of the handbag a bit narrower.

"Why are you making it so skinny?" I ask, watching her place the paper pattern onto the plastic.

"It wastes less fabric."

Then Mama starts to write the instructions on a piece of paper. Her handwriting is jerky and slanted. Finally she balls up the paper and throws it into the garbage.

"Why did you throw it away?" I ask.

"My handwriting is terrible. Kata, make sure you practice your handwriting."

"I already did." I show Mama the penmanship paper I got back from my teacher. On the top it has a "1," perfect, and no corrections at all. Then the number is crossed out, and there is a "5" in its place.

"Isn't '1' the best?" Mama asks.

"It used to be, but now they changed it to '5.'"

"Why is that?"

"To match the Great Soviet School System," I say, repeating the words of my teacher.

"Excellent," Mama says, looking closely at my small, even letters. "Kata, have you finished your homework yet?"

"Almost."

"Then do you think you could help me write these instructions?"

I look up quickly. Mama has never asked me for help before. "Are they long?"

"Not very."

"I'll try."

After dinner, Mama sits next to me and tells me what to write. *First, cut the pattern pieces on the dotted lines. Second, pin side A to bottom B and stitch.* I am careful to write straight across the wide paper in perfect cursive. The instructions are complicated.

"Do you need a break?" Mama asks.

I shake my hand. "No. But when we're done, can we write instructions for the bears? That way, when you are dead, I'll know how to make them."

"I'm not dead yet," Mama says.

"I know. But I still need the instructions."

"I have the pattern pieces," Mama says, pointing to a few sheets of tissue paper on the floor.

"I know. But I don't know all the steps."

"Okay. We'll write the bear instructions someday when we have more time."

I write the next step: *Cut two long strips 3 cm by 20 cm for the handle.*

"Where's Bela?" I ask as I copy.

"On an excursion," Mama says.

"For how long?"

"He said it would be about three days."

"Why didn't he tell me he was leaving?"

"Maybe he was in a hurry."

"He could still have told me."

"He must have forgotten."

It is ten o'clock when Mama and I finish writing the instructions for the handbags.

"Thank you, Kata," Mama says.

"Tomorrow we can write the instructions for the bear," I say.

"If we have time," Mama says.

I put my pajamas on quickly and get under my covers, but I cannot sleep. My right hand is throbbing from writing so much. If Bela were home, he would massage it for me. He would tell me how lucky I am that I have beautiful handwriting and a talent for drawing. But who even knows where my brother is now.

9

Eva is just coming out of her apartment when I pass her door. We head down the hill together.

The tall girl who was in the garden with Eva is waiting at the streetcar stop. She smiles at Eva.

"Hi, Zsofi," Eva says in a voice that sounds higher than usual. The girl has red lipstick on. My mother would never let me wear makeup. Eva puts her arm around Zsofi's shoulders and now they are whispering. I say bye, but Eva doesn't even notice that I'm leaving.

The wind is chilly and damp. I pull my jacket tightly around me and stuff my hands into my pockets. People are hurrying on the crowded sidewalk. A lady bumps me off the curb and I trip. My knee is bleeding a little. The lady doesn't stop. She doesn't say sorry. It seems like forever before I finally get to school.

Our teacher is telling us about the history of Hungary, and how the Magyar people have always had to fight for their country, their language, their very lives. It's hard to pay attention to her monotonous voice droning on. Outside the window, snow is blowing around. I think of Auntie

Erzsi, sitting by the woodstove, knitting hats and gloves and scarves. She made one for me and one for Bela. She taught me how to knit, but I think I've forgotten how to get started.

Finally the teacher dismisses us for recess. I go with my friends Zsuzsi and Anna and we huddle together in the front hall.

"Who cares about all that history?" Anna asks. She shakes her head and her blond curls shine in the sun. "Hey, smell this," she says, putting her wrist under my nose. I sniff, but I don't smell anything.

"What?" asks Zsuzsi.

"Perfume," Anna says. "My sister gave me a tiny dab. It's called Spring."

"You're lucky," Zsuzsi says to Anna. "Your sister's nice. Mine won't even let me look at her stuff."

"She's nice only when she feels like it," Anna says. "What about your brother?" she asks me.

"He's nice most of the time. Except he's hardly ever home."

"Where is he?" Zsuzsi asks.

"On an excursion."

"I wish I had an older brother," Zsuzsi says. "My little brothers drive me crazy."

"They're so cute," I say.

"Yeah. Since they're not yours. And besides, your brother is so handsome." She is blushing.

•

The teacher is reading the biology book out loud to us. I wish she would let us read it by ourselves. Her voice puts me to sleep, and she doesn't seem like she even understands what she is reading. I wish we still had our last year's teacher, Mrs. Kertesz. She told us that if you really want to accomplish things, you have to do more than memorize facts. You cannot accept things without asking why. For example, the discovery of penicillin was really an accident. Some mold grew in a dish, and instead of throwing it away, some scientists decided to see what mold really is. Why does it grow? they asked themselves. From that question, they made a discovery that has saved thousands of lives. But Mrs. Kertesz is no longer teaching at our school. When I asked Mama, she said that many teachers were forced to retire to make way for the younger teachers who have been trained in the new educational system.

I doodle on my paper. The teacher is reading about the parts of the cell. I guess everything is made out of cells, but then why do some cells become skin and some become hearts and some become ears? When Bela comes home, I'll ask him. Three days, Papa said. That means today he will be back. He didn't say what time. It could be early or it could be late.

"Kata," the teacher says.

I stand up.

"What is in the center of the cell?" she asks.

"The nucleus."

"You may sit down," she says. I can tell she is writing a

"1" in her grade book. My stomach turns over. A "1" means I failed. I have never failed before. I am the best student in our class. Did she ask me something else?

Then I see the teacher look at me, erase the "1," and put a "5" in its place.

The snow has turned into slush. I run the whole way home, take the stairs two at a time, and burst into our apartment. "Bela?" I shout before I've even crossed the threshold.

Mama is sewing.

"Is Bela home yet?" I ask.

Mama shakes her head.

My stomach drops. I was sure he would be waiting with his arms open, ready to swing me around.

"Kata, your stockings are covered with mud. Couldn't you try to avoid the puddles?" Mama asks.

I look down. Who cares about muddy stockings when you are hurrying home to see your brother?

"Now eat your soup."

"I am not hungry," I say.

"Eat a little, Kata," Mama says. "Something hot to warm your stomach."

"I'll wait for Bela."

"He may not even come today," Mama says. "He said *about* three days, not exactly."

"Three days is three days," I say, staring at my soup.

The doorbell rings. I know it's not Bela because he would never ring the bell. Maybe it's Eva. I look through the glass window and two ladies I've never met are standing there. Mama opens the door.

"Sorry to bother you," one lady says. "I am Irene. Your son Bela is a friend of my Jancsi's."

"And my Andras," the other lady says.

"Of course, of course—come in," Mama says.

The ladies sit on our sofa. Mama asks them if they would like a cup of tea, but they say no. "We have something important to discuss with you," the one named Irene says. She looks at me and smiles. "Maybe this is not for the ears of a little girl."

"Kata, go to your room," Mama says.

I do as I'm told, but I leave the door cracked. The lady named Irene says that her son Jancsi has not been home for three days. Neither has Andras.

"Bela said they have a three-day excursion," Mama says. "They should be back today."

"Excursion to where?" Jancsi's mother asks.

"I don't know exactly," Mama says. "Somewhere in the hills around Buda."

"I asked the leader of their study sessions, and he doesn't know anything about an excursion," Irene says. She takes Mama's arm. "We are so worried."

"Maybe there is another youth group. That's what it must be," Mama says. "There are many different youth groups all over the city." She looks at my door. "I'm sure they'll be home tonight. Or if not tonight, tomorrow."

Jancsi's mother stands up. "We are so sorry to bother

you. But please, if your son comes back, let us know right away." She hands Mama a piece of paper with her address on it.

Mama pats her arm. "Come anytime, even in the middle of the night, if you need something."

"Thank you," the lady says. Then she leans on Irene and they leave our apartment.

As soon as I am sure the ladies are gone, I run out of my room. "Mama, where is Bela?"

"I told you. On an excursion."

"But where?"

Mama's voice is sharp. "Kata, I don't know exactly."

Tears come to my eyes. Where is my brother? He has never even been gone overnight before.

I have homework in every subject. I start with the easiest, geometry. Usually I like drawing the small figures with my ruler, but today, my lines smudge and I have to redraw them three times. Then comes Russian, which I hate. The teacher is so old, he hardly knows what he's talking about. He was a prisoner of war in Russia during World War I, so he acts like the Russian-language expert when all he knows is the alphabet. He makes us copy dumb poems by someone named Alexander Pushkin that we can't under-stand at all. Mrs. Kertesz always told us to ask lots of ques-tions. I wonder why they said she was too old to teach when she was the best teacher I ever had.

I copy the first verse and look out the window into the

dark. My brother Bela is out there somewhere along with his two friends. They are on an excursion. But who knows where? When we were at Auntie Erzsi's, I never had to look for Bela because he was always in the house. But now I cannot find him.

Across the street I can see the lights on in some of the apartments. Then there are more buildings behind that. And finally I can barely see the hills of Buda.

The door of our building clicks. It could be him. It has to be. I hold my breath.

Papa is home.

10

Papa has stopped going to work. Mostly he sits at the kitchen table, reading. Sometimes he makes notes about the books on scraps of paper left over from the handbag patterns. When he is tired of reading, he goes and lies down on Bela's bed.

Uncle Sandor comes over for a game of chess, but Mama says that Papa is not well.

"What's the matter?" Uncle Sandor asks.

"The doctor said it's some sort of a … of a …" Mama glances at me. "A depression."

Uncle Sandor shakes his head. "Things are not easy for anyone." He takes a deep breath. "It will get better. Give him time. And let me know if I can be of help."

After Uncle Sandor leaves, Mama goes into Bela's room and shakes Papa's shoulder. He is lying in the bed. "You have to get busy with something," she tells him. "You cannot spend all day going from the couch to the bed."

Papa sits up. "I am studying."

"Yes, I know. You are studying. But what about work?"

Papa stares at the floor. "You remember how it was?" he whispers. His eyes meet mine. "Do you remember when you were a baby, Kata?"

Mama grabs his hands in hers. "Of course she cannot remember. A baby cannot remember." Mama puts her hands on Papa's shoulders. "You have to stop now. Please, Papa."

"I used to be the owner, Kata, do you remember? Sometimes I took you to the factory and carried you around on my shoulders. I showed you all the gears coming out of the big machines." Papa swallows hard. "They took my business. They cut my salary so that it is barely enough for one person, let alone a family. Next they will tell us that our apartment is too big, and we can keep only one room."

"Not necessarily," Mama says.

Papa looks at me. "Kata, do you remember all the machines?"

"A little."

"Gears are the building blocks of every machine. Even my watch has gears."

"She already knows that," Mama says, squeezing her lips together. I wish Mama would let Papa talk. He is so happy telling me about his factory.

"Kata, do you still remember when we had four rooms?"

I look at the wall behind the sewing machine. I know it used to have a door, and behind the door was a study lined with bookshelves. Bela used to sleep in that room, and Auntie Mari slept in the storage closet where Bela's bed is now. But I can't really remember how the room looked. "A little."

"Do you remember all the books?"

There was a book of poems on the bottom shelf by Jozsef Attila. Papa's favorite one was called "Mother." He said that it reminded him of my grandmother. I look at Papa and we recite the first verse together by heart:

"I thought of mother all the week each day,
I thought of her and stopped upon my way.
A squeaky basket in her hands she went,
Up to the attic with her shoulders bent."

Mama drops her arms and sits down at the sewing machine. I wish she would listen to the words and smile the way she used to. She knows all the verses to the poem. She could join in. But Mama isn't listening. When we finish reciting the last line, she says, "Kata, I need another copy of the handbag patterns and instructions."

"Why?"

"One for us, and one for Agnes and Lily." Then in a low voice she says, "I may have to ask them to help me with the sewing."

"What about the bears?"

"I will make the bears myself. But Auntie Klari thinks the handbags will be easier to sell."

The door of the building clicks open and somebody rings our bell. It is the supervisor from Papa's job. Mama does not invite him in. "My husband is not well," she says.

The man's voice is so low I can hardly hear. "I have come to tell him that it would be wise to report to the meeting tonight."

"But my husband is sick."

"I am just telling you that it would be wise."

The man leaves, and Mama goes to the bed where Papa is asleep. "That was your supervisor."

"And you told him I am sick," Papa says with his eyes closed.

"Yes, I told him. And he advises you to go to the meeting."

"Now they are forcing sick people to go?"

Mama pats my father's arm. "It was nice of him to come," she says. "He is trying to help you. Here, we'll wrap cloth around your throat. You tell them that you have had tonsillitis, but thank goodness, it is getting better."

Papa nods.

"And tomorrow you will be back at work."

"Yes. Tomorrow I will go to work," Papa mumbles.

Papa stays at the meeting so long. Mama keeps looking at the clock.

"Time for bed, Kata," she says.

"I have to copy one more page," I say.

"It can wait until tomorrow."

"I can finish now." *Number one, quilt the plastic by putting two identical pieces together with batting in the middle and stitching diagonally across the fabric, forming a diamond pattern. Number two, lay the pattern pieces onto the quilted fabric and trace around them with chalk.*

Slowly I write the sentences in my best handwriting. Finally I finish the page, blow on the ink, and hand it to my mother.

"Thank you, Kata. Now get ready for bed."

"Mama, what is a depression?"

"It is when you are sad—for a long time."

"Sad for what?"

"That depends. There could be lots of reasons. Now go to bed, Kata."

"Mama, is somebody really trying to take part of our apartment?"

"I'm not sure."

"We can always go to Auntie Erzsi's. Remember, she told us we could come anytime."

"You are right, Kata. Now go to bed."

"I want to visit Auntie Erzsi again soon. And I want to stay long enough to see all the animals."

"Okay, Kata."

"When can we go?"

"Soon, Kata, we will visit."

"You always say that."

I take my clothes off quickly, pull on my pajamas, and get under my covers. Mama says yes we will write the instructions for the bear, yes we will visit Auntie Erzsi, yes I will make a bear for you. But when? I can make my own bear. And I can take the train to Visegrád by myself.

BACK HOME   *March 1945, Visegrád to Budapest*

Auntie Erzsi is so sad when we go back to Budapest. She cries while we pack our things. We promise that we will visit her as soon as we can. Auntie Erzsi says she wants to keep me there on the farm like her daughter. I say good-bye to the big goat. I tell the goat that her next baby will not die. Mama says, Thank you, thank you for saving my children. Auntie Erzsi wipes her eyes with a handkerchief and pats my head. There is nothing to thank, she says. They are sweet children, these two.

On the train Bela asks, Are you sure the war is over? Mama says of course she is sure, but Bela is still scared. Outside the window of the train buildings have fallen down. Bricks are everywhere in big piles.

Auntie Mari is waiting for us. She says she is sorry there is so little in the stores. She could not cook a decent dinner. She says Papa will come home soon. A lady and her son are living in our apartment, but they use only two rooms so we can have the other two. The glass in the windows is all broken, so Auntie Mari has covered the windows with cardboard to keep out the wind. Our apartment is dark. There is a can with a fire in the middle so we can warm our hands and boil water. Auntie Mari has some meat and Mama cooks it on the kerosene stove, but it smells bad. I'm hungry, so I eat the meat, but I close my eyes and chew without smelling.

After we eat, Auntie Mari tells Mama that she hid the

sewing machine in the basement. It's still there, just dusty, that's all, but really it's as good as new. Mama hugs Auntie Mari and they are both crying.

There is shouting coming from the apartment below. I sit up. Could that be Eva's voice I hear through the floor? Something hits the wall and breaks. Maybe they dropped a plate or a glass. That must be it. Eva's father has such a loud voice. "You will go, you will go," he shouts over and over. I cover my head with the blanket.

Tomorrow Eva will come get me and we'll go to the Young Pioneers again. Sometimes the meetings are too long, but I like the singing part and the crafts. I like to take the streetcar with Eva and wear the red Pioneer scarf. Comrade Toth is sometimes mean and sometimes nice, but usually she pats my head. I hope that tomorrow is one of her nice days.

The door clicks. I hold my breath. It must be Bela. His footsteps are light on the stairs. The front door opens.

"That was a long meeting," Mama says.

"Ridiculous," my father says.

11

The weather has turned so cold that we run from the streetcar stop to the school. Comrade Toth is in a very good mood. When we come in, she says, "Kata, Eva, I'm so glad to see you." She teaches us a new song with three-part harmony. She asks me to demonstrate each part in front of the group. The song comes easily to me.

"The verses are hard to remember," one girl says.

Comrade Toth's expression changes quickly. "It only takes practice," she says.

She makes us sing the song until our throats are sore. We don't do any crafts because the song takes so long and we have to plan our excursion. Maybe Bela will be back when I get home. Maybe we can go find mushrooms, the kind that Papa likes so much. Then we will have mushroom soup and laugh and talk.

Eva pokes me. Comrade Toth is standing right in front of me. "Thank you for leading us in the song," she says. "I'm sorry some of the girls didn't catch on very well."

"You're welcome."

She pats my head. "Your curls are so pretty, Kata."

"Thank you."

"You are a very clever girl." Comrade Toth smiles with her big teeth like the wolf in Little Red Riding Hood. Sometimes Papa says, *Kata, I'll eat you up,* but then he hugs me in his big arms. "How would you like to sing a song on a stage one day?" Comrade Toth asks.

I don't know what to say. "I have to ask my parents," I say finally.

"Of course we will ask your parents. They will be happy to have you sing for an adult meeting." She turns to the group. "The meeting is adjourned," she says, moving toward the door.

On the way back, Eva leans her head against the dirty window of the streetcar. There are big dark circles under her eyes.

"Are you okay?" I ask.

"Of course I am okay," she snaps. She wipes her face with her hands. "You would be tired too if your parents yelled at you half the night."

"What are they yelling about?" I ask.

"They want me to go to every single Pioneer meeting, even the ones before school. Then when I go, they say I'm not active enough. Be a leader, Eva, they say. Now they want me to go to leadership training. Whatever I do, it's never enough." Eva covers her eyes with her hands. "They don't even like me anymore."

"I'm sure that's not true," I say quickly.

"How do you know?"

"Maybe they are just busy. My mom is so busy she hardly listens to anything I say."

Eva nods. "I don't know why people even have kids if they don't want them around."

"At least you like the Young Pioneers, don't you?"

Eva doesn't answer. She is playing with the red scarf around her neck. She looks like she really might start crying right there on the streetcar.

"Anyway, it's important to help the people, to help our country," I say, playing with my scarf.

"I wish my parents would help me," Eva whispers.

When I get home, Mama is staring at a postcard.

"What is it?" I ask quickly.

She hands the card to me. *We are fine. Please don't worry. Lots and lots of kisses, Bela.* I turn the card over. There is no picture on the front. The postmark says, *Wien. Österreich.*

Mama has tears running down her cheeks. "He made it, he made it," she whispers, pulling me so close that I feel her tears in my hair.

I don't understand. Why did my brother send us a postcard from Vienna? "When is he coming home?" I ask.

Mama shakes her head.

I pull away. "When is he coming?"

Mama is holding my arm, but I jerk away and run into my room and throw myself onto my bed. My brother is gone and he left me behind, he left me with Mama and

Papa. Auntie Erzsi was right. She told me that boys are like that, that they leave their families when they grow up. She told me but I didn't believe her.

Mama is stroking my hair. "He will send for us," she whispers. "Someday he will send for us."

I push my mother's hand away. "You knew. I know you did, but you didn't tell me."

I cry until my pillow is soaking and my eyes are so swollen I can hardly open them.

SEARCHING   *June 1945, Budapest*

After the war, Papa looks for his sister and his mother. Every day he goes to this office and that, searching lists of names. He goes to the train station. Sometimes I go too, and we watch all the people step out of the train cars. I've forgotten how my aunt and my grandmother looked, so once I say, Papa, it's them, but it's not. Papa pulls me the whole way home. Maybe they are far away, Mama says. Someday they will come home again. Or if they went to another country, they will send for us. Just wait, Papa, wait.

Mama is still there, stroking my back. I want her to stop. "You knew he was leaving," I say again.

"I knew."

"Did Papa know?"

"No."

"Why didn't you tell us?"

"Kata, try to understand." Mama is squeezing my hand. "It would have been too dangerous. What if somehow you let it slip, and then they caught Bela at the border? There are soldiers there, Kata. They would have killed him. And now he is free."

Then I am shouting. "Bela is a selfish brother. He left me here. He lied to me and you did too."

"No, Kata." Mama's voice is firm. "You are too young to understand. Your brother will send for us." Mama swallows hard. "You will see, Kata, someday we will all be together again."

"Bela doesn't care about us," I shout.

Mama's voice is sharp. "Now you are talking nonsense, Kata."

"Why do you always tell me to be quiet? Why?"

Mama is whispering. "Kata, people are listening to us. Do you want Eva's father to hear what you are saying and send the AVO Secret Police to our apartment?"

"My brother hates us," I shout even louder than before.

Mama stands up quickly and leaves the room.

Tak tak tak, snip. Tak, tak, tak, tak. Another handbag. And another and another. Never a bear for me. I will make a perfect bear for myself, with golden fur and sparkling eyes, and one for Eva too. Eva will say, *Kata, that is the most beautiful bear in the world.* She will take my arm and we'll sit on the garden wall.

Then I will take the train to visit Auntie Erzsi on the

farm. I will show her the bear that I sewed and together we will embroider handkerchiefs and dish towels and napkins. We'll gather flowers to put in the vase on the table and braid each other's hair and feed the goats. That's what we'll do.

As soon as Papa comes home, Mama hands him the postcard. His eyes move quickly over the words. "Good," he says.

"Did you know?" I whisper.

"I had some idea."

"Mama knew," I say.

"Is that right?"

I nod.

"Mama knows everything," he says softly.

I bury my face in Papa's sweater. "Bela is gone," I sob.

12

In the morning, Papa does not get out of bed.

"He has a headache," Mama says.

I look at my reflection in the mirror. My eyes are puffy from so much crying. My throat is dry. "I don't feel good either," I say.

"Wash your face and get ready." Mama fixes me a big cup of cocoa. Then she says, "Kata, don't tell anyone about the postcard."

I look down.

"And if someone asks, just say that Bela is on an excursion."

I gulp down my cocoa as fast as I can and run out the door. Mama thinks she can tell me exactly what to say and what not to say. *Tell them your name is Voros Kata, not Steiner Kata, do you understand? Never, ever say Steiner. Don't tell anyone about the handbags or the bears or the postcard. Tell them your brother is on an excursion.* What if I tell Comrade Toth that my brother escaped across the border? She will smile at me and write it down in the notebook. She will tell me what a good citizen I have become.

Or I can tell Eva, *We got a postcard from Vienna—from my brother Bela.*

The morning air is cold. I should have worn my heavier coat, but there isn't time to go back. I look around for Eva, but lately she's been leaving early. She says there are morning study sessions at school even before classes start. That's why she is so tired all the time.

I walk past the greengrocer and the butcher shop. An old lady is sweeping the sidewalk with a twig broom. Each time she makes a small pile of dirt, it blows away and she starts over again. Dust is blowing into my eyes and making them water. I wipe my face with my sleeve. I can't start crying or everyone at school will ask me what's wrong. The words of the Young Pioneer song are in my head. *Work is honor and glory. Work is honor and glory.* I say it over and over again as I walk.

Our teacher gives us a dictation. The sentences are long and complicated. Usually I don't have any trouble. Words just stay in my head and Hungarian spelling is easy. But this time, for number four, I have written only the first three words. It starts out about a beautiful bird in spring, but then it says to beware of something. Beware of brothers who don't tell you where they are going. Beware of comrades with big teeth. Comrade Toth is nice to me, but sometimes she's mean to the other girls. Like the other day she told Eva that she shouldn't eat so much because she is getting too fat.

The teacher is already on number five. But what about

the rest of number four? I try to peek at the paper of the girl next to me, but she has her arm covering it.

"Kata, keep your eyes on your own work," the teacher says.

The blood rushes to my cheeks. I know what everyone is thinking. Steiner Kata, the best student in the class, is cheating. The blister on my finger pops and blood gets onto my paper. I try to wipe it off, but it smears. I put my finger quickly into my mouth and the teacher is already on number seven.

At our snack break, I stand with Zsuzsi and Anna.

"The dictation wasn't too hard," Zsuzsi says.

"I think I got them all right," Anna says. She turns to me. "What about you?"

"I missed a few."

"Eva told me you've been going with her to the Young Pioneers," Anna says. "Is it fun?"

I nod.

"What do they do?"

"Sing songs and make flags."

"Is it like the Little Drummers?"

"Sort of. Except our scarves are red, not blue."

"You already got a red scarf?" Anna asks.

I nod.

"You're lucky," says Zsuzsi. "I can't wait until next year when we can all be Pioneers."

"My sister said the Young Pioneers have discussions," Anna says.

"Just a little," I say. "Mostly we plan trips."

"Trips to where?" Anna asks.

"Hiking trips around Budapest," I say.

"You mean excursions," says Anna.

I try to change the subject. "I wish I'd brought a bigger snack. I'm starving."

Anna offers me a piece of her bread.

"Hey, my sister said your brother hasn't been coming to the youth group meetings. She said she misses him," Zsuzsi says.

"He's on an excursion," I say, almost choking on the bread.

Zsuzsi pats me on the back. "Are you okay?"

I cough again. "I swallowed wrong," I manage to say.

The afternoon drags on. In math, we have to copy a whole sheet of geometric figures. My finger hurts where the blister popped, so my lines are light and shaky. In geography, we draw maps of the Soviet Union and its allies again, only this time we have to add all the rivers and major cities. I know where Vienna is, but that's not one of the cities we're supposed to draw because Austria is not an ally of the Soviet Union. When I get home, I'll look in Papa's atlas and draw my own map of Austria. I know Vienna is in the eastern part, on the Danube. That means the same water that flows by Budapest flows by Vienna too. But I'm not sure which way the water flows. If I put a stick in the Danube, maybe Bela will see it from the bridge in Vienna. Or maybe if he writes me a note and puts it into a bottle, I'll find it on the banks of the Danube here in Budapest.

The air is cold but the sun is warm. I decide to take the long way home from school. I want to see my favorite chestnut tree on the corner of Katona Jozsef Street and Pozsonyi Road. There it is, even bigger than I remembered it, with its bare branches stretching out over the street. In spring, the buds will get fat, and then the little leaves will pop out, five to a stem. Bela and I used to watch them grow, and then came the big white flowers, and finally the wild chestnuts that we gathered. My eyes are still stinging from yesterday. Why didn't Bela tell me he was leaving? He knows I wouldn't tell anyone. He knows I can keep a secret.

NAMES   *June 1945, Budapest*

Mama says I am Steiner Kata again. But what if someone knows that we are Jewish?

That's okay now, Kata. Jewish or not Jewish, it doesn't matter anymore.

But the boys on the farm said they threw rocks at a dirty Jew to make sure he would never come back. They said Jews kill babies and drink their blood. Can I stay Voros Kata now? Please? I never told anyone my real name. Never. I promise.

Shh, Kata, it doesn't matter. You are Steiner Kata, okay? That's the name you had when you were born.

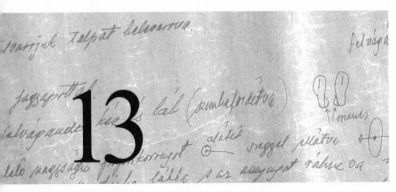

13

When I open the front door, Andras's and Jancsi's mothers are there with Mama. All three of them are staring at Bela's postcard.

"He didn't mention our boys," Irene says.

"I am sure they are all together," Mama says. "They left together. They will stay together."

"But why didn't we get postcards?"

"You will," Mama says, patting Irene's arm. "You know how the mail is these days. Look here. It says 'we' are fine."

Irene's eyes are red. "Maybe Jancsi and Andras didn't make it. Maybe they got split up somehow. You never know."

Mama strokes her back. "You'll see. Everything will be all right."

"And there's another thing. What do we say about our sons when people ask? That they disappeared? That we don't know where they are?" Irene asks.

"We say that they went on an excursion," Mama says.

"But after a while, people will begin to wonder."

"Then we can say that we have no idea."

The other lady shakes her head. "People don't just disappear," she whispers.

"These days, anything can happen," Mama says.

"Now at least our sons are far from here," Irene whispers.

The ladies stand up and Mama helps them put on their coats. "Thank you for the tea," Irene says.

"Let me know if you get any news," Mama says.

"Certainly. We will."

"And stop by anytime," Mama says.

Mama sits down at the sewing machine to make handbag handles.

"Did Andras's and Jancsi's mothers know that they were planning to leave?" I ask.

Mama turns the handle around and runs a seam down the other side. "No, Kata, they didn't." She doesn't look up from her sewing.

"I bet they told their mothers they were going on an excursion."

"Probably."

"I wish Bela had taken me with him."

Mama looks up from her fabric. She opens her mouth as if she is about to say something, but no words come out.

Scraps of plastic and lining and wool are all over the floor. I scoop them into a pile. The yellow wool from the bears is soft and fuzzy. I will save up the scraps to make my own bear. I'll watch Mama carefully to see how she sews in the brown paws and inserts the metal disks at the leg joints.

"Are you going to make more bears?" I ask.

"Yes. I have two new orders."

"From whom?"

"Imre's friends."

"And the rest of the orders are for handbags?"

Mama nods.

Papa is sitting at the table with his book open, but he isn't reading. He has his head in his hands. The doorbell rings and there is his supervisor.

"Comrade Steiner," the man says to Papa. "Would you like to come with me to the meeting?"

"My husband has a headache," Mama says.

The supervisor looks worried. "I'll take care of him," he says softly.

Mama looks at Papa. He stands up slowly and gets his hat and jacket, and together he and his supervisor leave the apartment. I watch out the window. Papa is so stooped he really does look like a grandfather.

14

Papa has been waking up at five o'clock every morning and going to study sessions before work. When he comes home in the afternoon, he barely says a word.

"Papa, today it is a bit warmer," Mama says. "Why don't you go out for a walk?"

Papa shakes his head.

Mama raises her voice. "Please. At least help me a little."

"What help do you need?" he asks.

"Go get some meat. I hear there is beef over at the butcher shop. And go next door to the greengrocer for green beans too. There must be some fresh ones by now. And don't bring any cabbage. Last time I got cabbage there, it was full of worms."

Papa stands up.

"Kata, go with Papa. Help him carry the packages."

I take Papa's hand. I want him to smile. I want him to stop at the park, but I know he is in no mood for that and I am too old to be pushed on the swings. The warm wind is blowing and I start to take off my jacket.

"No, Kata," Papa says.

"But it's hot."

"All we need is for you to get a sore throat." Papa pulls the jacket up on my shoulders.

We are passing the park. Two girls are swinging double. One is sitting and one is standing behind her, pumping. They are probably sisters. Bela used to pump my swing so high that for a minute we were weightless and I shrieked, *Slow down,* and he said, *Come on, Kata, let's fly.*

We join the line of people at the butcher shop. A lady taps Papa on the shoulder from behind. "Matyas, it's been so long since I've seen you," she says. "And this must be little Kata, so big already."

"Yes," Papa says, kissing the lady's hand. "How have you been? And how's the family?"

"Fine, just fine," she says. I have no idea who the lady is. "What is Bela doing with himself these days? He must have graduated already—is that right?" she asks.

Papa's eyes dart around the shop. The lady is waiting for an answer. It's a simple question. All Papa has to say is, yes, my son graduated. Papa is turning his head every which way and shifting his weight from side to side. The couple in front of us look at him strangely. The lady repeats her question. "Didn't Bela graduate last year?" Everyone in the store is looking at us.

"Bela is … Bela is …" Papa repeats. But he cannot finish his sentence. His face is white. He is swaying on his legs.

"My brother is looking for a job," I say to the lady.

"I see."

"But right now he is on an excursion."

"How nice," the lady says. "He can enjoy this lovely spring weather."

Papa has moved out of the line.

"And my father has been sick," I say. "He has had a very sore throat. Tonsillitis, I think."

"So sorry to hear it. As the weather warms up, I hope he feels better."

"Yes." I nod at the lady.

"Don't you want to get back in line?" she asks.

"I think we'd better go," I say. "Papa needs a cup of tea."

"Can I pick something up for you?"

"No. No thank you."

The lady pulls her brows together. "Yes, you had better get him home."

Everyone is looking at us. Some people are shaking their heads like Papa is crazy. Others are whispering. They feel sorry for me, a little girl with a crazy father. I take Papa's hand, and we slip out the door.

I pull Papa along. The street is crowded and he bumps into a man on the corner. "Watch where you're going," the man says, shaking his fist at my father.

Papa seems not to notice. He is looking down and I am pulling him up the hill. But my father is too heavy. Twice I have to stop and catch my breath. At the corner near our house, Papa stops once more. "I'm sorry, Kata," he says softly. "I don't know what happened. My mind is not—I am not thinking clearly."

"Sometimes that happens to me too," I say, squeezing my father's hand.

He takes a deep breath. "I'm sorry, Kata."

As soon as we get home, Papa stumbles into Bela's room and flops onto the bed.

"What happened?" Mama whispers to me.

I cannot talk. I cannot tell my mother that my father is a crazy man who can't answer the simplest question. Mama pulls me close, but I turn away and head toward my room.

"Kata."

I don't turn around.

"Please, Kata. Tell me."

Mama's voice is begging. I look back. She drops the head of a bear onto the floor and the sawdust stuffing spills out. Papa is snoring on the bed. "He couldn't even answer a simple question," I say.

"What question?"

"Where is Bela?"

Mama shuts her eyes. She stands in the middle of the room like a statue.

I kneel down, scoop the sawdust into a pile, and start stuffing it back into the bear's head. The poor bear had all his brains spilled onto the floor.

"We will think of something," Mama whispers.

"But what?"

I take a needle and thread and stitch the head shut. I make the stitches tiny so that the sawdust cannot come out.

"You sew very nicely, Kata," Mama whispers.

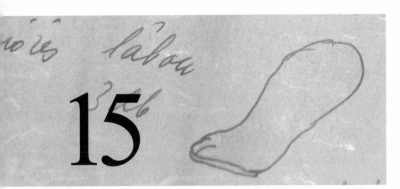

15

It is past midnight, but still I cannot sleep. The click of the sewing machine is soft, so I know Mama is not stitching the plastic. I get up and stand at the door of my room. Mama is sewing together the three parts of a bear's head.

"Kata, you should be asleep," she says without looking up.

"I woke up."

"The sewing machine is too loud," Mama says.

"I like the sound it makes," I say. Mama sews down to the tip of the nose and snips the thread.

"Can I help you make this bear?" I ask.

"You should be asleep."

"But I'm not tired."

Mama looks at her watch. "Okay. For ten minutes you can help." She hands me the bear's head. While she starts on the arms, I stuff the head with sawdust. Finally the head is firm. Mama feels it. "A little more," she says. I add another handful. Then we hear Papa groan from Bela's bed. Mama gets up and looks at him from the doorway. "A bad dream," she says, coming back to the sewing machine.

"Sometimes I have bad dreams too," I say.

"Everybody does."

I want Mama to ask me about my bad dreams, but she doesn't. I want to tell her that I dream about looking for her and Papa at the train station. There are so many people, but none of them are my parents.

"I thought of a plan," Mama says. "Tomorrow afternoon Papa and I will go back to the butcher shop. Then I will shout at Papa so everyone can see that he is deaf. Nobody would expect a deaf man to answer a question about his son."

"But people will wonder why he wasn't deaf before."

"Sometimes people become deaf."

"Why is that?"

"Ear infections, scarlet fever. There are lots of reasons."

"Mama?"

Mama doesn't answer.

"Maybe Papa is crazy."

Mama looks up quickly. "Never say that again, Kata," she says sharply. She cuts the thread with her teeth. "Papa is tired. Very tired. He needs to rest."

She is moving the treadle so fast, guiding the fabric underneath the needle. Her mouth is in a thin line. I want to say sorry for what I said about Papa, but there is a lump in my throat. It takes me a long time to finish stitching up the head of the bear. "This one will be the star of his class. I think his name is Wilhelm," I say finally. "Isn't that a good name for such a smart bear?"

Mama doesn't answer.

"How about Wilhelm?" I ask again.

"Kata, sometimes you act like an eight-year-old." Mama takes out a crooked seam and sews it over again. "I told you so many times, I don't think you should name the bears."

"They name themselves."

"Don't be ridiculous."

"Well, they do."

Then Papa is there, standing in the living room with his eyes closed. "Go back to bed," Mama says.

"I want to tell you …"

"Go to sleep, Papa. You are very tired."

"I want to tell you …" Papa looks at me. "Thank you, Kata," he mumbles.

"For what?" I ask.

"For … for …" Papa cannot find the words in his head. I want to help, but I'm not sure what he means to say.

"For bringing you home?" I ask.

"Yes, for … for … the butcher …"

Mama takes Papa's hand and leads him back to Bela's bed. I wait for her to come and finish the bear. I clean up the table top and put everything into neat piles. Finally I look into Bela's room, and Mama and Papa are both lying on the narrow bed. Mama is on her stomach with her arm across Papa's chest. I watch Papa's slow breathing and Mama's arm moving up and down with each breath. Papa's eyelids twitch for a minute. Maybe he is dreaming, a good dream about finding mushrooms in the forest.

IN THE FOREST *August 1945, Outside Budapest*

Papa takes us into the forest to look for mushrooms. He knows where to find them and which ones are poison and which ones are good to eat. What if you make a mistake? Bela asks.

Papa knows, Mama says. Trust him. Don't you want mushrooms for dinner?

My stomach is growling. Every day Mama makes patties with old flour and water. They are hard to chew and they taste bitter. But today we are going to have mushroom sauce. Is this one okay? Papa nods. Pick it carefully, Kata. Put it into the basket.

Like this?

Papa smiles. We are picking mushrooms together in the forest.

I go back to the bear and arrange the legs on either side of the body. The only thing left to do is assemble all the pieces. I've watched Mama many times before. The metal pins go through the holes in the disks. I pick up the pliers and pull the pin though the washer in the arm. Then I twist the ends. The arm moves up and down just right. I attach the other arm and the leg. The head is harder. The neck is stiff. I have trouble fitting the pin through the hole. Finally I twist the ends and Wilhelm is finished.

It is almost two o'clock in the morning. I want to sleep with Wilhelm. I know Mama doesn't like me to play with the bears. She's afraid they'll get dirty. She thinks I am much too old to play with stuffed animals. But just this one night won't hurt. Mama won't even know. I shake off the loose sawdust and carry Wilhelm to my bed.

I hear shouting coming from downstairs. "You will do what I say," a man's voice shouts. "You will go."

I hold Wilhelm against my stomach and shut my eyes. The voice is definitely Eva's father's. Maybe Eva is hiding under her covers. Maybe she is staring her father right in the face. I wonder if she has a stuffed animal that she holds.

"You will obey your father," he shouts. I can hear every word as if he were in our apartment. What if Eva's father is hitting her? I hold my breath and wait. A door slams and a drawer shuts. Something falls to the floor and breaks. The shouting has stopped.

Outside the window, the sky is light purple. The streetcar is loud as it turns the corner of our street. Soon the sun will rise. I tiptoe over to the sewing machine, set Wilhelm on the table, and go into the bathroom to wash my face.

Mama has the cocoa and bread ready as usual. "Kata, you look tired," she says.

I take a sip of the cocoa and look up. There are dark circles under Mama's eyes. "You too."

"You must have stayed up half the night," Mama says, looking over at Wilhelm.

"I couldn't sleep."

Mama looks out the kitchen window. "Thank you, Kata, for finishing the bear. Thank you very much."

16

At school I can hardly keep my eyes open. I doodle in my notebook. I write my name with a big fancy *K*. Then I draw a bear like the one I will make for myself out of scraps. He will have nice round ears and shiny glass eyes. He will be pieced together, so there will be extra seams here and there. That's okay. I think I will name him Miklos, but Imre's bear that he calls Bruni is really Miklos, so maybe I should use a new name. I'm not sure. I'll have to see the bear before I can give him a name.

Zsuzsi pokes me. All the other kids are closing their notebooks. Time for a quiz.

"Draw a map of the Soviet Union and its allies," the teacher says. "Then draw all the major rivers, lakes, mountains, and natural resources."

I know exactly where to put the Matra Mountains. We used to go there in the summer with our cousins and pick wild berries. Mama and my aunt made the best jam in the world.

The teacher is collecting the papers and I haven't added any of the rivers yet. Quickly I draw the Danube passing by

Budapest. The teacher is coming closer. Which way does the Danube turn? I draw the familiar bend, and then I put in a black dot and label it *Vienna*.

"Kata," the teacher says, looking at my map.

I stand up to answer.

"Can you name the allies of the Great Soviet Union?" she asks.

"Hungary, Romania, Yugoslavia, Czechoslovakia, Poland," I say.

"Is Austria one of our allies?"

"Not Austria."

"Then why did you put Vienna on the map?" The teacher puts a "1" in her grade book.

I feel the blood rush to my face. If only I had Mrs. Kertesz again. She never made us memorize maps. She explained to us why the political boundaries of Hungary changed so often throughout history. First there was the Austro-Hungarian monarchy under Franz Joseph. When it fell apart, the boundaries were drawn. "Why?" I asked. Her face lit up. *The only one who is ignorant is he who does not ask*, she said. Then she explained everything with a story.

But this new teacher cares only about having us memorize everything, and it seems that the only thing she's interested in is the Great Soviet Union. Mama says that's part of the new educational system, but whatever it is, it's boring. I look down at the floor and count the tiles.

•

The sky is bright blue and the buds on the trees are fat. Spring is my favorite time of the year. Fall is nice too, but you know that winter will follow. In spring, you have the whole long summer to look forward to. If Bela were here, he would take me to the big swimming pool on Margit Island. He would race with his friends, and my friends would say, *Look at your brother. He is such a good swimmer. His shoulders are so wide, so strong.*

Nobody is home when I open the door of the apartment. I heat soup up for myself, cut a slice of bread, and eat quickly. It's quiet without the sound of the sewing machine. Where is Mama? Then I remember. She and Papa are going to the butcher this afternoon to pretend that Papa is deaf. What if it doesn't work? What if nobody believes their story? What if somebody already knows that my brother has left the country?

The door downstairs opens. If it is the AVO, I will tell them that my brother doesn't live here anymore. He moved out a while ago. He didn't get along with my parents and now we don't know where he is.

I hear Mama's voice in the stairwell. She is holding Papa from behind, pushing him up the stairs. Once they are inside the apartment, she guides him toward Bela's room. "Now rest, Papa," she says. "Rest a little."

My father slumps over onto Bela's bed. Mama helps him lie back on the pillow and covers him with a light blanket.

"Mama."

Mama puts her finger to her lips. "Shh, Kata. Let Papa rest."

"But Papa does not really have tonsillitis," I say in a normal voice. Then I turn to my father. "Papa, let's go to the park this afternoon."

Papa doesn't answer. His eyes are closed. I want to shake my father and tell him that there is nothing really wrong with him at all. But Mama takes my hand and pulls me out of the room.

Mama is sewing and I am collecting the scraps from under the table. She says that everything went according to plan. When she entered the store, she shouted, "Papa, do you want to get pork or veal today?" Papa didn't answer. She asked him again, even louder. Finally he said, "Whatever you want." Mama told the butcher that Papa has had tonsillitis and several ear infections that have left him very hard of hearing. She hopes it is temporary, and that soon he will be able to hear again. The butcher said what a shame, and hopefully time would help. Everyone in the store heard. One lady said to try peroxide. It helped her husband.

"What did Papa say?" I ask.

"Papa is deaf. He said nothing."

For a second I think my mother is telling me the truth.

17

Eva comes to get me for the Pioneer meeting. Mama is sewing furiously. "What's your mother making?" Eva asks when I open the door.

"A handbag."

Eva is looking around our apartment. She sees the bears on the table. "They're so cute," she says. Then she lowers her voice. "Where's Bela?"

"Not home."

She looks disappointed. "Maybe he'll be here when we get back."

"I don't know."

As we head out the door, Eva whispers to me. "I have a secret to tell you, Kata. But don't tell it to anyone else."

"Okay."

"Do you swear?"

"I swear."

"I don't know if I should tell even you."

"Come on."

"Do you promise not to tell anyone?"

"I already promised."

"And you have to tell me all your secrets."

"Okay."

Eva takes a deep breath. "I'm in love with your brother."

"Bela?"

Eva grabs my arm. "You only have one brother, don't you?"

"But Bela ... is so old."

Eva tightens her grip. "Older and wiser," she says. "You are lucky to have a brother like that."

"He's hardly ever home," I say.

"Well, I've been thinking a lot about it, and I think maybe you can help me arrange a ... rendezvous."

"A what?"

"A rendezvous."

"What's that?"

"A secret meeting."

"I don't know anything about that."

"You can be the one who arranges the meeting."

"My brother is ... very busy—I mean he's hardly ever home."

"Well, when he is," she says, "I can just 'drop by.'"

Finally the streetcar comes. It's not crowded, but we can't find seats together. I glance over at Eva. Her forehead is covered with pimples. Her cheeks are big and round. Can she really be in love with my brother? She hardly even knows him. Don't you have to know someone to be in love? Sometimes people fall in love with movie stars. But then, at least they've watched the movies.

•

As soon as we get to the meeting, Comrade Toth pulls me up to the front and asks me to sing the song she taught us the week before. I sing each part separately, and then she asks two other girls to join me in three-part harmony. One of them doesn't remember all the words.

"Practice for next week," she says, frowning. She says it to all three of us, even though only one girl forgot the words. Then she tells us to divide into groups and come up with ideas about how we can make the country stronger, cleaner, and brighter.

"We can pick up garbage," I say.

"Good idea," Comrade Toth says. "But you have to think of more."

"We can purge ourselves of those who do not contribute to the ideology of the Hungarian Workers' Party," Eva says.

I don't know what she's talking about. First she wants a "rendezvous" with my brother and now she's talking about "ideology."

Comrade Toth says that is a very good idea too. She asks Eva to explain.

"We have to find those people who don't believe in our ideas and get rid of them," Eva says.

Comrade Toth nods. I wonder if Eva means get rid of the people or get rid of the ideas. How do you get rid of someone? For a minute I think about Papa in Bela's bed, snoring under the thin sheet. Did the Hungarian Workers' Party already get rid of my father?

It's crafts time. Today we can make whatever we want, like flags or cards. I take the paper and cut out a rectangle. I'll make a card to send to Bela. On the front, I make a bear. I cut the pieces carefully, glue them into place, and draw the black eyes and nose with a pen.

"He's so cute," Comrade Toth says, holding up my bear for everyone to see. Then she takes him and says it is time to go home. I want my bear card back, but I'm afraid to ask. Now she's smiling at me with her big wolf teeth. "Kata, I talked to my leader about you."

"Your leader?"

"Yes. My leader. And he invites you to come and sing for us in two weeks."

"Thank you, Comrade Toth. Who will sing the other two parts of the song with me?"

"Just you. You can sing the melody by itself."

I swallow hard. "I'll ask my parents if I can go," I tell her.

On the way home, Eva is quiet. Finally she says, "I don't think Comrade Toth likes me at all."

"That's not true," I say.

Eva looks as if she might cry. "I don't think I should have told you about Bela."

I take her arm. "That's okay."

"You won't tell your brother that I told you, right?"

"I promise."

She smiles a little. "Kata, you are my only friend in the whole world."

"You have other friends," I say, remembering the tall girl.

"I mean a real friend."

"You have your parents too."

"All they ever do is order me around. When they're home, that is."

"My parents are like that too."

Eva looks up. "Your parents are always home. And I never hear them shout."

"I mean they order me around too. My mother does. All my father does is sleep."

"I wish my father would sleep. Instead he yells and throws things and says that I am a lazy girl who will never amount to anything." Eva's eyes are watery. "Just because I don't want to wake up at five-thirty for a meeting every single day of the week." We open the gate to our building. "So when do you think your brother will be back?" Eva asks.

For a minute I want to tell the truth. Eva says I am her best friend. Her only real friend. I told her I would tell her my secrets. All I have to say is "My brother left Hungary." *Don't ever say your old name. Don't tell anyone about the postcard.* I swallow. "I'm not sure."

"Don't forget the rendezvous," she whispers.

"I won't. But my brother is on an excursion."

Eva narrows her eyes. "He has to come back some-time."

"He's very busy, you know, organizing Pioneer groups all over the country."

I am about to go into our apartment when Eva grabs my arm. "Hey, Kata, I have something else to tell you." She is pulling me into the corner of the stairwell. "Don't tell anyone ..." She looks around. "Your brother kissed me."

She lets go of my arm and runs up the stairs.

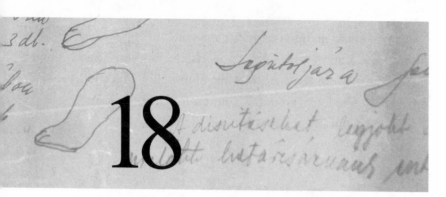

18

There have been no more postcards from Bela. When I mention his name, Mama looks around like someone might hear us through the walls. She sews furiously all day and into the night. Some days Papa goes to work and some days he stays in Bela's bed. When he gets up, he reads. His hair is getting long and he doesn't even think to brush it. One day Mama shaves it off with a razor so Papa looks like a bald old man.

I sit at my desk and doodle. I write my real name, Katalin, with a big fancy *K*. Underneath it I write my middle name, Edit, after one of Papa's sisters who died of polio. I saw a picture of her, with dark eyes like Papa's and mine, and curly hair. I wish she were here, and my little curly-haired cousin too, so I'd have somebody to play with. Eva has avoided me ever since she told me that Bela kissed her. I bet that's because it's not even true. She just made it up.

I open the window. The spring air is warm and damp. I breathe deeply. There's a good smell coming from downstairs. I wish we had meat almost every day like Eva's family. Mama said they have connections, but what does that really mean? Eva told me that their apartment has three big rooms, one for her, one for her parents, and one more for sitting and reading in. I try to remember the way our apartment used to be with the study full of books. Papa kept the poetry books on the bottom shelf so that I could reach them. I couldn't really read, but when I saw the first line, often I could recite the rest. There was one poem by Petofi Sandor about a tree that I especially liked. *Listen, Mama,* Papa used to say when I took out the book. *See. Our Katika can read.*

I want to write a letter to Bela, but we don't have his address. We don't even know where he is right now. I could write to Auntie Erzsi and tell her I'm sorry that we haven't come to visit in a while, but then what will I say? That I hope to visit soon? I want to write to somebody my age. I want to write about Eva and how she says I'm her best friend, but I'm never sure if the things she tells me are true or not. I want to write about how my brother Bela left me all alone.

I take out a piece of thin paper and write the date on the top: *6 April 1949.*

Tak tak tak. Mama is sewing again. I decide to write to the bear that I'm going to make. He doesn't have a name, so I write, *Dear Bear.* Starting on the next line, I write, *I know Bela would never do anything as disgusting as kiss Eva. I think she just made it up. Bela is not that kind of brother. Of course, I don't know what kind of brother he really is. He could at least have told me he was leaving. He could have said good-bye.*

The doorbell is ringing. I fold the paper, shove it between two books on the shelf, and hurry to open the door. There is Irene. "Is your mother home?" she asks.

As soon as Irene sees Mama, tears start running down her cheeks. "You won't believe what happened." Irene takes out her handkerchief and wipes her face. "The AVO called me in."

"And?"

"They said they had evidence that my son has escaped. They asked me if I knew anything about it."

"What did you say?"

"That I didn't know anything." She swallows hard. "And then they said that only a terrible son would abandon his parents. They kept repeating that. 'What kind of a son wouldn't tell his mother where he was going? What kind of a son lies to his parents?'" Irene is crying again. "Then they asked me if he went alone. I said I didn't know. They kept asking me, over and over." She wipes her eyes. "And I still said I didn't know."

Mama is rubbing Irene's back.

Irene takes a deep breath. "They said I am free to go home and think about it, and come back when I remember."

Mama puts her arm around Irene's shoulders and holds her close. Irene is sobbing. "You did very well, very well," Mama says.

"But they will call me again."

"Shh. They let you go. Everything is okay. And the main thing is that our boys are safe."

Suddenly Mama remembers that I am there. "Kata, go get a glass of water for Auntie Irene, and then go to your room."

Irene's hands are shaking so much that she can hardly hold the water to her lips. "You are a sweet girl," she says, trying to pat my head.

I try to listen to Auntie Irene and Mama through the closed door, but they are talking so softly that I can catch only a word here and there. Then Irene is crying again.

I go back to my room and open my math book. I do my geometry problems and then start on geography. I study the map of Europe in case we have another quiz tomorrow. There is the Danube. I trace the blue line with my finger. On the other side of the Danube and west a little bit is Austria, where Bela is waiting for us. I measure the distance with my finger. It is not far at all. The key says each centimeter is fifty kilometers. That means Vienna is only about two hundred kilometers. In Vienna they speak German. Suddenly I realize that when we join Bela, all my classes will be in German.

I take a German book that my uncle gave me off the book shelf. It is about two little naughty boys, Max and Moritz. They get in trouble and have their eyes pecked out by chickens. I can understand the story from the pictures, but I can't read the words. What am I going to do in Austria if I can't speak German? I will ask Papa to start teaching me.

Auntie Irene is gone and Mama is sewing again. I sit on the sofa and hold the two newest bears on my lap. One of them has an alert look like Wilhelm. The other one looks a bit sleepy.

"This one is called Albert," I tell Mama, "because his eyes are bright like Albert Einstein."

"I see," Mama says, turning the lining of the handbag inside out.

"And this one is called … let's see, what is a sleepy name? How about Matyas, like Papa? Matyas is a sleepy name."

Mama snips her thread and looks up at me. "Kata, please."

"But they cannot go out into the world nameless," I say, hugging them both. I go into my room and sit at my desk. I take out a scrap of the yellow plastic and my best fountain pen. Then in fancy cursive on the plastic I write *Albert* and underneath it *Matyas*. I cut out the names into little squares and make small holes near the top.

"I made name tags for the bears," I say, showing my mother.

"Kata, you do not listen to me."

"A name tag won't hurt. If they don't like it, people can take it off," I say, tying the tags around the necks of the bears with pieces of red ribbon. "But at least they'll know what the names are supposed to be so the bears won't end up with dumb names like Bruno."

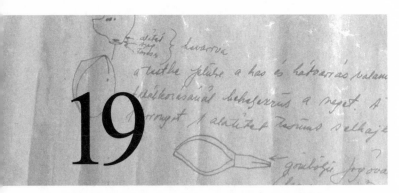

19

Auntie Klari comes to pick up the handbags and the bears, but only four handbags are ready.

"We have to fill the orders in a timely fashion," she says, "or we will lose all the customers."

I want to tell Auntie Klari that my mother has been sewing nonstop every day, but I'm not supposed to interrupt.

"How about hiring other people, as I suggested last time?" Auntie Klari asks.

Mama turns up the volume on the radio. "I was trying to avoid it." She lowers her voice. "You know how the Hungarian Workers' Party feels about people having employees, and I am sure some of our neighbors are watching us. But you are right. I simply cannot do all the sewing myself."

Auntie Klari nods. "A few people to help you with a little sewing—I would not call them 'employees.' They are friends, that's all, friends who will help you make gifts, if anyone asks."

"You are right," Mama says. She takes out the patterns and instructions from her desk drawer.

"And when do you think the handbags will be ready?"

"In another week or so."

Auntie Klari nods. "I'll tell the clients that a fine hand-made product is well worth the wait."

"Do you want to take the bears today?" Mama asks.

Auntie Klari sees them sitting together on the sofa. "Oh, they are so cute. And name tags, how wonderful."

"It was Kata's idea," Mama says. "Take them off if you like."

Auntie Klari considers. "You know, I like them with the tags. It makes them seem more ... personal." She looks closely at the names. "How did you decide on Albert and Matyas?"

Mama looks at me.

"I don't know," I say.

Auntie Klari smiles. "You have a good imagination, Kata."

I hope Auntie Klari will leave the bears with us until the handbags are ready. I especially wish she would leave Albert. But she is holding them in her arms.

"And tell me, how is your grandson?" Mama asks.

"Much better," Auntie Klari says. "You were right. The warm air has helped." She takes a deep breath. "Maybe the warm air will help your husband."

Mama shakes her head. "I don't know."

Auntie Klari looks around our apartment. "Where is Bela these days? I haven't seen him in a while."

I wonder if Mama will tell the truth. Auntie Klari has

known us for a long time. She used to babysit for Bela when he was little. But Mama says, "He is on an excursion."

"I see," Auntie Klari says. She reaches into her handbag. "Here. Take these." She hands Mama a small plastic bag with dried apricots. "They have so many vitamins. They will help your husband."

"Save them for your grandson."

"Please, Etus, take them. Your husband needs his strength during these hard times." She touches my mother's arm.

Tears come to Mama's eyes. "What is there to do?"

"Only one thing," Auntie Klari says. She lowers her head. "Get out of this place." Then she speaks so softly I can barely hear. "Is Bela on a permanent excursion?"

Mama nods.

"And have you heard from him yet? Is he all right?"

"Yes. He is … across the Danube."

"Then someday you will join him."

"Yes. Someday."

"But me, I am stuck here forever." Auntie Klari stands up and smooths out her skirt. In a regular voice she says, "Okay, I'll be back next week for the handbags and the bears."

"Thank you, Klari. For everything." Mama holds up the small bag of apricots. They are shriveled and brown. "Thank you."

Auntie Klari opens the door to leave. For a minute I think I see Eva in the hallway, but then she is gone. It couldn't have been her. What would she be doing, standing in the hallway outside our apartment?

"Etus," Auntie Klari says, bending over to kiss my mother. "Everything will be all right."

"Yes. I'm sure it will," Mama says.

Mama shuts off the radio and sits down at the sewing machine as usual. "Comrade Toth asked me to sing at a meeting," I tell her.

"Is that right?" Mama is concentrating on the bear's ear instead of on what I am saying.

"I mean an adult meeting on Thursday night."

Mama pulls her eyebrows together. "Is Eva going?"

"No. Only me," I say.

20

On Thursday after dinner, I help Mama clean up the living room. I gather up all the fabric scraps and sweep the snippets into the garbage. We put all the plastic fabric and handbags on Mama's bed and cover them with a blanket. Now nobody can tell that Mama is selling anything.

When Comrade Toth comes to pick me up, I introduce her to my mother. Papa is sleeping in Bela's room.

"Thank you for inviting Kata to sing," Mama says.

"Your daughter has a lovely voice," Comrade Toth says, smiling.

"Not a talent she inherited from me," Mama says. She straightens out the bow on one of my braids. "Now you'd better get going or you'll be late."

"Of course." Comrade Toth takes my hand.

On the streetcar, she asks me if I am sure I remember all the verses of the song.

I nod.

"And do you understand it in your heart?"

I'm not sure what she means. It is a song about a boy who

works so hard that he dies and brings honor to his people. I like the melody much more than the words. "I think so," I mumble.

"If somebody asks you about the words of the song, will you be able to answer the questions?"

"I think so."

"And remember to call everyone 'Comrade.'"

"I'll remember."

The meeting is in a big room in the basement of an office building. When we get there, people are standing in small groups, talking. "Hello, Comrades," they say to us. Comrade Toth introduces me to everyone as "my little friend."

When the meeting starts, a lady says that at the end of the meeting there will be a special treat. Then she begins with something called self-criticism. A man goes up and says that he took a three-hour lunch break when really he should have taken only two hours. The lady writes down what he says. He lowers his head, he is so ashamed. He says that now he will work extra hard to make up the lost time. Next a lady says that she bought makeup on the black market even though she knows it is illegal and wrong. She will not do it again. Black market. Isn't that exactly what Mama is doing with the bears and the handbags? I feel a lump growing in my throat.

The meeting is long and boring. I put my hands together, cross my middle fingers, and turn my hands so my fingers make a seesaw. Bela taught me how to do that.

Comrade Toth holds my hands still. "Kata, pay attention," she whispers. The lady is saying that there is a very talented little Comrade here who would like to sing us a song. Comrade Toth leads me up to the stage. There are steps on the side. I hold on to the railing and walk up by myself. She says, Don't forget the words, Kata. She smiles but her teeth look like the big bad wolf.

I take a deep breath and sing from my stomach the way my music teacher taught me.

"Once there was a boy named Ivan,
He was so sweet, this Ivanka,
So good.
He worked hard in the fields
Toiling under the hot sun
Every day."

I stop to take a breath. Sweat is dripping down my back. Poor Ivan must have been even hotter than me. I want to take off my sweater, but everyone is watching me.

"But Ivan didn't keep what he grew,
He gave it to those
Poorer than himself.
Not so his parents.
They hid extra food
In the cellar.
But Ivan took it out

And said to the people,
Here, this is for you.
Ivan got so thin,
Poor boy,
But still he worked
For the people.
Then one day,
Poor boy,
He couldn't get up,
He couldn't walk.
His friends brought him soup
But alas it was too late
For poor Ivan."

I hold the last note as long as I can. The audience is quiet, and then they clap. I turn to look for the stairs. Where are they?

One man stands up. He looks familiar, with his blond mustache. "Very good," he says. "Thank you for a wonderful performance."

I don't say anything.

"I have one question," he says. "Do you know Russian?"

The man's voice is familiar too. A loud, raspy voice. It is Eva's father. "A little bit, sir."

"Then why didn't you sing the song in Russian?"

I look for Comrade Toth, but I can't find her wolf teeth in all those people. "I don't know, sir," I say.

"Comrade."

"I don't know, Comrade. But if you'd like, I can learn it in Russian."

"So you study Russian?"

"Yes, sir."

"Comrade."

"Yes, Comrade."

"There is one more thing. Where are the parents of this talented girl?"

"My parents are at home," I say. "My father has tonsillitis and my mother has to take care of him."

"I see," he says, sitting down.

Where are the stairs? I can't find my way down. Finally a lady points to the railing on the side. I shift my weight back and forth like Papa at the butcher shop. "Over there, little girl," a lady says. Then I see the railing and I stumble down the stairs. Comrade Toth does not come to get me. Maybe the song was wrong. Maybe my voice was off pitch. Finally she takes my hand and pulls me out of the building.

It has started drizzling, but we don't have an umbrella. We walk as fast as we can to catch the streetcar. Comrade Toth is reading a pamphlet. On the cover is a girl on a tractor, smiling. Her cheeks are pink and her hair is blond. *Work Is Our Future,* it says on the top.

On the streetcar, Comrade Toth looks upset. "I should have taught you the words in Russian," she says. "The man was very disappointed."

"He's always disappointed," I say.

She pulls her eyebrows together. "Do you know him?"

"He's Eva's father."

Comrade Toth sucks in her breath. "Really? I had no idea."

"And he's always upset about something or other."

Comrade Toth looks down. "Still. I should have thought to teach you the song in Russian." Her voice sounds like she might cry. I am afraid to say anything more.

When I get home, Mama is sewing. "How was it?" she asks.

"Okay."

"You were gone for a long time."

"Eva's father asked me why I wasn't singing in Russian."

"Eva's father was there?"

"Yes. And he asked where my parents were."

Mama stops the treadle. "What did you say?"

"That my father has tonsillitis and my mother is taking care of him."

"Very good, Kata," Mama says. "You are a very clever girl. You always know what to say."

"But I forgot to call him Comrade."

"What did you call him?"

"Sir."

"Next time try to remember."

"If Comrade Toth asks me to sing again, I'm going to say no."

"It's better to do what she asks," Mama says. "Remember, we want to join Bela."

"I don't care."

Mama looks up. "You don't care about joining Bela?"

"I don't want to sing for those people ever again," I say, going into my room and shutting the door.

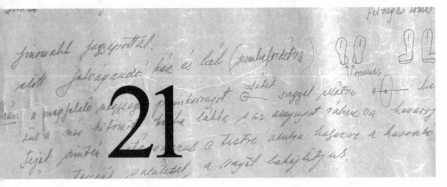

21

In the morning, Mama and I head around the block to where Lily and Agnes live in their small apartment.

"How do we know Lily and Agnes?" I ask.

"They used to clean Papa's office," Mama says.

"Do they have husbands and children?"

"Lily was married. But her husband died, so the two sisters live together."

Lily and Agnes are happy to sew the handbags. "This plastic is very nice," Lily says. "Very modern."

Mama shows them the patterns and the instructions that I copied. They review each step. "Let me know if you have any trouble," Mama says.

"I hope our machine will take this plastic," Lily says. She sits at the machine and tries a sample piece. The needle moves along easily.

"No problem," Agnes says, smoothing the pattern pieces under the desk lamp. "When do you need them?"

"A week or sooner, if you can," Mama says.

Agnes nods.

"Sew a handbag for yourselves if you wish," Mama says.

"Thank you, Auntie Etus." Agnes smiles and I see that many of her teeth are missing. She holds her hand over her mouth. "The extra money will be very welcome."

Mama sighs. "For all of us," she says.

Lily offers me a piece of candy. "No thank you," I say.

"How is school?" she asks me.

"Fine."

"And how's that big brother of yours?"

"Fine," I say, smiling.

She looks over to the mantel, where there is a framed photograph of a young man with a mustache. "If only my Zoli were here." She shakes her head. "No sense in looking back, isn't that right, Etus?"

"That's right," Mama says, and we leave the apartment.

We are quiet as we walk. The wind is warm and damp. We pass the park with the swings, but nobody is swinging. There are puddles of muddy water everywhere. People are standing in line in front of the stores, blocking the sidewalk. Mama stops for a minute to see what they are trying to buy. "A radio, I think," she says. "Papa would love a new radio." She looks in her purse and counts the forints. Then she shakes her head and we push our way past the crowd of people.

When we get home, Mama sits down to sew right away. I gather the scraps under the machine.

"Mama, why do you tell some people where Bela is but not others?"

Mama stops sewing. "We have to be very careful," she says.

"But you told Auntie Klari."

"She is an old friend."

"What about Lily and Agnes?"

"The fewer people who know, the better."

"What if the AVO asks me? What should I say?"

"They will not ask a child."

"But what if they do?"

"Tell them that your brother is on an excursion."

"Are people really watching us?"

"They could be."

"What are they watching for?"

"That is hard to say, Kata."

The doorbell rings. Eva is there with the red scarf around her neck. "Hi, Kata. Are you ready?"

I forgot. We have a Pioneer planning meeting. "I'll be ready in five minutes," I say.

Eva stands there, looking around. Her eyes settle on the handbags by the sewing machine. Then she glances at the back room and I know she is looking for Bela.

"My brother is not home," I tell her.

She blushes. "I'll be back when you're ready."

When the door closes, Mama is pale. "I only hope Eva couldn't hear us talking through the door," she whispers. "She could tell her father everything we said. From now on, Kata, we have to be more careful."

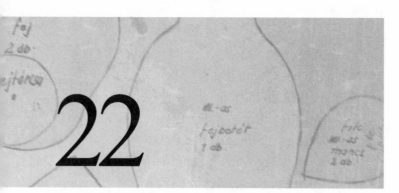

22

The wind is so strong that it blows us sideways. A garbage can has turned over and trash is blowing everywhere. Eva grabs my arm as we head to the streetcar stop. "So, tell me about your brother."

"What about him?"

"Like, what's his favorite movie?"

"I don't know."

"What's his favorite book?"

"I don't know that either."

Eva puts her mouth close to my ear. "How about his favorite cologne?"

"I have no idea."

Eva lets go of my arm. "Don't you know anything about your own brother?"

"Of course I do."

"Well, tell me something then."

Suddenly I don't know what to say. Why should I tell Eva anything about Bela anyway?

"Hey, has he ever had a girlfriend?"

"Yes, lots," I say quickly.

"Like who?"

"Zsuzsanna, Ella, Baba."

"What did he do with them?"

"He took them to the movies, wherever."

"You're making that up. I never saw him with a girl."

"No. It's true. Lots of girls like Bela."

"I know. But they weren't his girlfriends." Eva takes a deep breath. "Hey, Kata, did you ever see him kiss one of those girls?"

I blush. "No."

Finally the streetcar comes.

We plan the excursion. We will be divided into four groups. One group will bring drinks, one sandwiches, one dessert, and one snacks. Each group will perform a skit that will teach part of the Workers' Party ideology to the others. My group has Eva and three other girls. We are supposed to teach that it is important to distribute resources equally among the people.

"Like everyone should have an apple. Nobody should get two apples and leave someone without any," Eva says.

"But what if somebody doesn't like apples?" asks one girl.

"Then her apple can be divided up."

The girl nods. We plan a skit about a greedy girl who takes everything for herself. Then, one day, her friend finds a whole stash of candy in her book bag. She explains to the girl how important it is to share the candy with everyone.

The skit is boring. I wish I had some candy right now. Eva doesn't want to be the greedy girl, and neither do the other two, so that is my part. At the end I have to say, "I am sorry and now I understand."

"Say it like you mean it," Eva says.

"But I don't."

"What do you mean?"

"I'm not really greedy," I say.

"Then why did I see four handbags at your house? A person needs only one."

"They are for our friends," I say quickly. Then I repeat the line. "I am sorry and now I understand."

On the streetcar home, Eva and I don't say a word. Her cheeks are red again and she has so many pimples. I'm lucky I don't have anything like that on my forehead.

"Why are you staring at me?" she says finally on our way up the hill.

"I'm not."

I want to grab her braid and say, *Come on, Eva, let's play in the garden. I'll braid your hair any way you like. I'll make it look so pretty.* Just before her door, Eva stops.

"You didn't say anything to anyone, did you?"

"About what?"

"You know."

"I told you I wouldn't."

"I just want to make sure."

•

When I open the door, Mama is holding another postcard.

Dear everyone,
    Don't worry because I am fine and making plans. I miss you and send you lots and lots of kisses.
    Bela

I read it over and over. I trace the letters of Bela's messy signature. Vienna is not far at all, just west and across the border. By train it would take only about four hours.

"When can we go?" I ask.

"Where?"

"To join Bela in Vienna."

"First Bela has to get on his feet wherever he is, and then he will send for us."

"He's in Vienna."

"Yes, for now." Mama looks at the postmark. "But who knows where he will end up."

My stomach turns. "What do you mean?"

"I mean that we will follow Bela someday, Kata."

"But why not now?"

"We could get caught by the border guards," Mama whispers. "It is not so simple to just go across."

"Bela did it, and Andras and Jancsi."

"But now it is even harder."

"Why didn't we all leave together with Bela?"

"Shh, Kata. You talk too loud." Mama puts her finger to her lips. "How was the meeting?"

"I could have gone with Bela," I say in a voice even louder than before. "He could have taken me."

"Kata, stop."

I drop the postcard onto the floor.

Mama is sewing again. Her hands guide the fabric and suddenly the needle goes down on her finger. Quickly Mama puts her finger into her mouth, but there is already blood on the fabric.

"Are you okay?" I ask.

Mama takes her finger out of her mouth, and a drop of blood forms quickly on her skin. She goes to the sink and runs it under cold water.

Papa stumbles out of Bela's room. "What's going on here?" he asks.

Mama turns off the water and dries her finger with a towel. "Mama stitched her finger," I say.

Papa holds Mama's hand close to the window. The bleeding has stopped. "Is it okay?" he asks. He gets a bandage from the cabinet and puts it gently onto Mama's finger.

I set the table for soup. Papa says Mama makes the best soup in the world. Mama won't smile or talk. Then Papa asks me about the meeting.

"We have to do a play," I say.

"That's nice."

"It's a dumb play. And they made me be the greedy one."

"Don't worry about that, Kata. It's just a play," Papa says. "And it sounds like you got the best part."

"Eva said we are greedy because we have so many hand-bags."

Mama looks up from her soup. "What do you mean?"

"She saw all the handbags."

"And what did you say?" Mama is holding her breath.

"That we are making gifts for our friends."

"Excellent," Mama says. She looks at Papa. "You know, that Kata of ours is a quick thinker."

"Like her mother," Papa says.

"I don't want to go on the excursion," I say.

"We'll see."

"But I don't."

"Kata, if you want to join Bela someday, you have to be a good Pioneer."

"Let her decide," Papa says.

Mama looks at Papa. "A child of eleven?" She picks up her bowl and takes it to the sink.

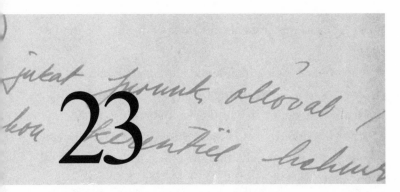

23

We pick up the handbags from Agnes and Lily, and Mama is pleased. The stitches are straight and sure. They followed the instructions perfectly.

Now all the handbags and bears are done, but one bear still has no name. She looks like a girl, this soft bear with the blue nose. She could be Lily, but it's too flowery. Matilda is better. I make a nice curly *M* on the tag.

"The name tags are wonderful," Auntie Klari says when she comes. "My boss loved them. She bought both bears for her nieces. You know, Etus, I was thinking that we should raise the price for the personalized bears."

"To what?"

"Twelve forints."

"Don't you think that's a little high? I mean, all we added was a name tag."

"It's the idea that people are paying for, Etus, not the tag itself. It's brilliant, really."

"Whatever you think."

"Yes. Twelve forints for a personalized bear." Auntie

Klari gives Mama a whole envelope of forints for the last order.

There is a knock at the door. "Hi, Kata," Eva says. "Do you want to play in the garden?"

At first I wonder if she has been standing outside our door for a while. Her eyes are darting all around. Greedy. Eva said we are greedy, but she's the one who has veal chops every day. "I have lots of homework," I say.

She steps into the apartment even though I didn't invite her in, looks around, and then shrugs. "Okay. But maybe later we should practice the skit."

"We already practiced."

"But not enough."

"Okay. Later."

"I'll be back in a little while." She looks around once more before heading down the stairs.

After Auntie Klari takes the bears and the handbags, Mama cleans up around the sewing machine. I gather a big pile of wool scraps. Most of the pieces are small. I take them into my room and sort them by size. I can use the bigger pieces for the body and head of my bear, and the smaller ones for the arms, legs, and ears. I still don't have quite enough fabric, but if I keep collecting more, it won't be long.

Mama stands at the door of my room. "Klari really liked the name tags," she says.

"Yes." I am rearranging the scraps on the floor.

"Thank you, Kata," Mama says.

I look up. "For what?"

"For insisting on naming the bears." Mama turns away and then back. "For being a stubborn daughter. Oh, and Kata, there's one more thing. I think you should practice the play with Eva."

"I'm busy now. I have things to do."

"You can do them later."

"It's a dumb skit."

"But still. I noticed you were not very friendly to Eva."

"She's not so friendly to me either."

"She's just being a teenager."

"I know."

"And her father has become head of the Hungarian Workers' Party in our district."

I swallow hard. "He has?"

Mama nods.

I put the scraps back into the bag and head downstairs. When Eva answers the door, her eyes are all red and watery. She says she cannot come out now because her mother has chores for her to finish. Her mother's voice is loud and angry. "Eva, you call this clean? Come here right now."

"See what I mean?" Eva whispers.

I nod.

"I'd better go." She shuts the door.

24

After dinner, Mama wants to take a break from sewing. "How about we all go out for coffee," she says to Papa. He is reading at the table.

"We can have coffee at home," he says.

"But it would be nice to go out, don't you think?" The window is open and the warm air is blowing the curtains. Mama takes a deep breath. "The air is so full of spring."

"And informers," Papa mumbles.

"Please."

"Why waste money that we don't have?" Papa asks.

"Look what I earned from selling the handbags and the bears."

Papa glances at the stack of bills in her apron pocket. "That is more than I earn in two weeks."

Mama puts her hand on his arm. "Once in a while we have to get out," she says.

Papa stands up slowly. "And if I meet my supervisor or my co-workers?"

"Then we will say hello and smile."

"And they will smile now and spit on me tomorrow."

Mama pulls Papa toward the door. "A little cup of coffee, one for each, will be nice."

"Coffee for Kata?"

Mama looks at me. "Coffee or cocoa?" she asks.

"Coffee," I say.

Mama takes my arm. "You know, Papa, our Kata is so grown up. She had a very good idea." Mama tells Papa about the bears with name tags, but it seems that Papa is barely listening. He has his eyes on the ground as we walk.

In the café, I decide on a cappuccino with whipped cream. Mama and Papa get espressos. Mama orders a sweet roll for us to share, but Papa doesn't even taste it.

"Try a bite," Mama says. "It's very good."

Papa shakes his head.

Two girls sit down at the table next to ours. One of them looks familiar, but I don't know where I've met her before. She sees me and smiles. "You're Bela's little sister, aren't you," she says. "I'm Judit. We met at the pool once."

"Oh, yes. These are my parents."

"Hello," Judit says, standing up to shake my parents' hands. "So, are you and Bela planning to swim again this summer?" she asks me.

"Yes. I think so," I say.

"See you then."

She goes back to her friend. My cheeks are flushed. Of course Bela will not take me swimming this summer. If I go to the pool by myself, everyone will ask, *So where's your brother?*

"A friend of Bela's?" Mama asks.

I nod.

Mama stirs her coffee with the small spoon and I see that her eyes are watery. Then she picks up the small cup, drinks the coffee in one gulp, and stands up to leave.

"Let's walk around the square a bit," she suggests.

Papa shakes his head. "It's getting late," he says. I don't want to walk around either.

Mama sighs. "Please, Papa, try."

Papa pulls away. "I am trying," he says through his teeth. "Isn't that enough?"

I take Papa's hand and we head slowly away from the square. When we get home, I take my Dear Bear notebook off the shelf, but what should I write? I draw a small picture of a bear. I draw a lot of bears in a row. Underneath each one I write the name. That way I'll remember all the bears we ever made.

SCHOOL   *September 1945, Budapest*

The room is cold, but we are so happy to be back in school. Sari, Agnes, Vera, and Vera's twin sister, Anna, sit in the first row. Then there is Zsuzsanna, Maria, Judit, and me. Our teacher calls the roll, and when our names are called, we say, "Present." Eszter is absent for a whole week. Is she sick? I ask Maria, but she doesn't know. Eszter is gone the next week too. When I ask Mama, she says Eszter is not coming back.

Why not? Is she sick?

No, Kata. Eszter and her mother were hiding in the basement and part of the building was bombed.

You mean the building fell on them? How do you know?

I heard from someone who knew them, someone else in the building.

Where is Eszter's father?

I don't know, Kata. I went to their old apartment and their furniture is still there, but another family is living in it. When I asked, they said they didn't know Eszter or her parents.

How can they not know them if they are using the furniture?

I tell our teacher that she doesn't have to call Eszter's name because she is not coming back. She doesn't ask me how I know or what happened to Eszter. She only takes a pen and draws a line through her name.

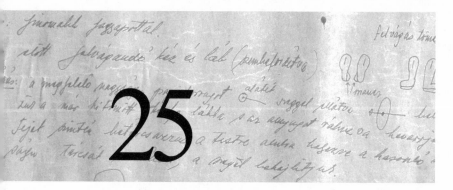

25

"They absolutely loved the name tags," Auntie Klari says when she comes. "You cannot even imagine how excited everyone at the office was when I showed them. They kept looking at the name tags and trying to decide which one they liked best." Auntie Klari has a list of new orders for five bears and three handbags. I want to stay home and help Mama sew, but she says I should go on the excursion with Eva.

"I don't like Comrade Toth," I tell Mama. "She takes my things."

"What things?"

"My pictures."

"Just try to get along with people, Kata," Mama says.

"I can tell Eva that I have a sore throat," I say.

"You cannot lie."

"We lie all the time. Anyway, my throat really does hurt a little."

"Kata, we have enough trouble with Papa." Mama is already laying out the pattern pieces.

On the streetcar, Eva says her cousin said Bela doesn't come to her Pioneer group anymore.

"That's because he's going around the country, helping people form new Pioneer groups," I say.

Eva narrows her eyes. "I think you're just trying to keep your brother from me. My cousin said nobody is going around the country."

"Maybe your cousin doesn't know what my brother is doing," I say, looking out the window.

"Hey, does your brother like poetry?" Eva says in a more pleasant tone.

"Yes."

She reaches into her book bag. "Then give this to him." She hands me a folded piece of paper.

"Okay. When he gets home."

The hike is long and hot. I want to stop and rest, but Comrade Toth says we have to be strong if we are going to make the country strong. She even wants us to sing while we walk up the hill. She takes my hand and pulls me to the front of the line. "You are such a cute girl, Kata," she says. Other kids hear her say that and I blush.

I'm glad to get away from Eva. She won't stop asking me about Bela—whether he likes chocolate ice cream or vanilla, whether he can dance, whether he's an early riser or late.

Finally we get to a field where we sit down and have a picnic. The dark bread tastes good with cheese. After lunch, we are supposed to form small circles. Then we will perform our skits. I don't want to be in Eva's circle, but Comrade Toth puts us together.

"Have you ever kissed a boy?" Eva asks one of the other girls.

She puts her hand over her mouth. "That's so disgusting."

"I don't think it is," says the redheaded girl.

"So, have you done it?" Eva says to her.

The redheaded girl looks around. "I had a boyfriend last year."

"And what did you two do?"

"Talk."

"And what else?"

"Hold hands."

"That's it?"

The girl nods.

"What about you, Kata?" Eva asks.

I don't answer.

"She's too young," says the redheaded girl.

"I've never been kissed," I say.

Eva takes a deep breath. "Well, I have." Her face turns red from the neck up.

"Who?" whispers the redheaded girl.

"I can't tell," Eva says.

"Well, I don't think kissing is so terrible," says the redheaded girl.

"It depends on how you kissed," another girl says.

"No, it depends on *who* you kissed," the redhead says.

"What do you mean?" asks Eva.

"Well, if you really are sure you love him, it's okay," the redhead says.

Comrade Toth is coming our way. She sits down on the blanket next to me and takes my hand. When she talks, her breath smells like cigarettes. "How are you girls doing?" she asks. "Are you enjoying the picnic?"

"Very much," says Eva.

"Are you ready for your skit?"

"I think so," says the redheaded girl.

One group shows a family huddled around a radio listening to the news from the West. They are telling all kinds of lies about what is happening in Hungary. Then one of the girls says everything the Western radio says is untrue, and that the Hungarian radio station broadcasts the news, pure and simple. We all clap. Next is our turn. I go around in a circle, hoarding all the candy. I don't want to share it with anyone. Eva says sweetly, "Don't you think you should share with those who have less?"

"No," I shout. "I want more." I start cramming the candy into my mouth. For a minute I forget that I am in a play. The sugar is sweet on my tongue. Then Eva comes up and explains that those who have the most must give to those who have less. In a socialist country, everyone is equal.

The girls all clap for us and I give everyone a piece of candy. Comrade Toth is very happy with our skit. She asks me to sing the song about Ivan for everyone, so I do, only I forget some of the words in the middle. Comrade Toth says I should review it for the next time I need to perform.

On the way home, Eva says that I really am Comrade Toth's pet.

"I don't think so," I say, even though I know it's true.

"She always wants you to walk with her and everything, just because you're cute and you can sing."

I don't know what to say.

"When you get older, you might not be so cute anymore," Eva continues. She reaches into her pocket and takes out a round, flat container of powder. "When you get older, you can wear makeup like this. Do you want to try some?"

"I don't know."

"I got it from Anna," she whispers. "Her mother has tons of it in her dresser drawer. Here, I'll put some on your nose," she says. She dabs a sponge full of powder on my face. Then she puts it on her forehead on top of the pimples. "Do you think I'm beautiful, Kata?"

"Of course," I say quickly.

She looks at her reflection in the window of the streetcar. Then she says, "I love the handbags and the bears your mother makes. You're so lucky."

"She isn't making them for me." After the words are out of my mouth, I wish I hadn't said them.

"I'm sure you can have at least one bear and one handbag, right?"

"I guess so."

"I mean, you have so many. Your mother must have lots of friends."

"I think you're lucky because you have a big apartment and you get to eat veal chops all the time."

"How do you know?"

"I can smell them."

"I'll bring you some leftovers."

"I don't think my mother would like that."

"You can eat in the garden and she won't even know."

"She'll know anyway."

"How?"

"My mother knows everything."

Mama has finished two more bears. I look at their faces, one so serious and the other one laughing.

"Antonia and Liliana," I decide quickly.

"Wouldn't shorter names be easier?" Mama asks.

"But those are their names," I say, starting on the fancy *A*.

"How was the hike?" Mama asks. Her eyes look tired and the wrinkles in her forehead are deep.

"Fine."

Mama smiles. "I told you it wouldn't be so bad."

I finish the name tags, tie them around the necks of the bears, and gather up the scraps.

26

Auntie Irene is at the door. "Etus," she says, practically falling into my mother's arms. "Now it's over."

Mama leads her over to the sofa. "What happened?"

"I told them that the three boys left together." Her voice breaks. "There was nothing I could do. They kept saying, 'If you tell us where your son is and who he went with, nothing will happen to you.'"

"Did you give them names?" Mama asks.

I hold my breath.

"I had to, Etus. I had to."

Mama is still patting her arm. I want to throw the bear arm that I am stitching at her. I want to push her out of our apartment.

Mama tells me to bring Auntie Irene a cup of tea. She keeps saying, "I'm sorry, I'm so sorry," over and over again.

Mama is quiet.

"The AVO officer said nothing would happen to us," Irene says. "I told him our sons are grown up. We cannot control them anymore. I told him that my husband is very active in the Hungarian Workers' Party."

"My husband is not," Mama whispers.

Finally Irene says she'd better get going. She tries to hug Mama, but Mama doesn't hug her back. Her arms just hang there by her side.

As soon as Auntie Irene leaves, Mama starts sewing. She is moving the treadle so fast that there is hardly any time between the *tak taks*. When Papa comes home, she barely looks up.

"The AVO knows about Bela," I tell him.

"What?"

"Auntie Irene told them," I say.

Mama finishes the handbag handle, snips the thread, and looks up. "She couldn't help it. They kept questioning her."

Papa stares at the floor.

"She shouldn't have told," I say.

"Kata, be quiet," Mama says.

"She shouldn't have," I repeat. "She didn't have to give them my brother's name." I am sobbing and talking at once.

Papa pats my head. "It's okay, Kata." Mama is sewing again.

"How about we say he died?" I say.

"Kata."

"We can say he died. Then they won't have anything else to ask."

The doorbell rings and there is Eva. She motions for me to come out into the hallway. "Did you give it to him?" she whispers.

I almost say, *My brother died,* but then I say, "Not yet."

"He's still on that excursion?"

"Yes."

Eva looks at me suspiciously. "Are you sure?"

"Of course I'm sure."

"You want to play out back?"

"My throat is getting sore," I say quickly.

"Okay. See you later."

I go into my room and read the letter that Eva has written to my brother.

My Dearest Bela,
I love you
with all my heart.
Please don't forget
the last kiss we had.
If only it could have lasted
Forever,
like the sun and the moon
and the stars in the sky,
forever and ever.
With love always,
your Eva

Could Bela really have kissed her? My brother would never have done that. I tear up the poem and throw it into the garbage can.

27

In the morning, Eva says she wants her poem back.

"I'll give it to you this afternoon."

"Did you lose it?"

"I thought you wanted me to give it to Bela when he gets home."

"I changed my mind."

"Okay. I'll bring it over."

That afternoon I look in the garbage can, but Mama has already taken out the trash. What will Eva do if I tell her I threw her poem away? I lie down on my bed and try to remember the lines. I know it started out: *My Dearest Bela, I love you with all my heart.* But what came next? Something about the kiss. Yes, that's it. And the sun and the moon and the stars. Quickly I scribble what I remember of the poem on a scrap of paper. It's missing something. The line about lasting forever. Yes, that's it. Now I think I have the whole thing.

I practice different kinds of handwriting. Eva's is round and small, but not too small. I write, *My Dearest Bela.* Too big. I try again. Too slanted. Eva's writing is straight up and down. I do it over and over until I get it right. Then I carefully copy the whole poem onto a small piece of paper and blow on the ink. How exactly was it folded? Into quarters? It looks too big. I fold it once more.

What if Eva says that's not her handwriting? I unfold the poem and stare at the words. Is there any way she could tell that it isn't hers? I think a corner was torn. I fold the corner of my copy and tear it off. There. It's perfect.

I knock at Eva's apartment. When she comes to the door, I thrust the paper into her hands.

"You didn't read it, did you?" she asks.

"Of course not."

"I decided not to give it to him."

I don't say anything.

"Don't you want to know why?"

"Why?"

"Because I'm not sure I love him anymore." Eva wipes her face with her hands. "There may be someone else that I love."

"I'd better go," I say, backing away from the door. "I have to pick up some milk for my mother."

Eva just stands there. She doesn't go in or out. "Kata?"

I turn back.

"I still like your brother. But love is more than that. You'll see when you get older."

I slip out the front door of the building. The air is almost hot. I walk quickly and sweat is dripping down my back. There is a long line at one of the shops. I slow down to look, but I can't see what people are waiting for. Probably something I don't need anyway, like nylon stockings.

I turn the corner and head toward the Danube. Bela and I used to walk to the Danube all the time. When my legs were tired, he carried me on his back.

I walk along the promenade. A couple is coming toward me. The boy has his arm around the girl. She looks up at him and smiles. They sit down on a bench. I look away toward the water. It is muddy today, and full of branches from all the rain. I walk down to the riverbank and look for a rock to skip. Flat, round rocks work best, the smooth kind, washed by the river. Bela showed me how to flick my wrist and make the rock jump like a frog. I let the stone go and it jumps fourteen times. I try again and again, but I can't get more than eight.

I'd better head back home. Mama will worry if I'm too late. The park bench is empty. The wind is blowing and people are hurrying to the streetcar stop. I push my way onto the streetcar, but I can't get a seat. The floor is wet and dirty. There is the smell of wet shoes and sweat and mud. It takes forever to get to the corner of Krisztina Street and Meszaros Street, where finally I make my way out of the streetcar and up the hill.

When I open the door of our apartment, Mama is sitting on the sofa, staring straight ahead.

"Mama?"

She doesn't move.

I go over and touch my mother's knee. "Mama?" A half-finished bear is dangling from the sewing machine needle. "What's wrong?"

"They took him."

"Who?" I am holding my breath. There are footsteps on the stairs. Bela has light steps, he moves so fast. Nobody can take Bela. I hear the click of Eva's door.

"Papa," Mama whispers. "They took him. The supervisor told me."

"Where is he now?"

"I should have let him stay home." Mama is sobbing.

THE BOSS   *November 1945, Budapest*

I stand on the balcony of my room and see Papa hurrying home. He walks fast, my father, and he is smiling. The factory is ours again. Steiner and Company, Gears and Wheels. Part of the building was destroyed by a bomb, but Papa and his friends have been working every day to clean the rubble. And finally, all of the machines are working again. Mama makes palacsinta pancakes for dessert to celebrate the good news. Our friends come over and celebrate with us. That is good news, they say. After so much trouble, things are working again. We are rebuilding the country. Papa has champagne that he pours in all the glasses, Bela's too and a little bit in mine. She is a child, Mama says. Papa smiles. One sip to celebrate. Cheers. Cheers for the future. We clink our glasses.

28

It is dark when I set the table with two bowls and heat up the soup. Mama isn't hungry. She puts the spoon to her lips, but the soup drips back into the bowl.

"Maybe somebody can help us," I say.

Mama pushes the bowl away, goes into Bela's room, and lies down on his bed. I follow her to the doorway. "We have to think of something," I say.

Mama shuts her eyes.

I wash the bowls and clean the counters. Then I sit at the sewing machine and finish stitching the body of the bear, the arms, the legs. The treadle is hard to reach and my leg is tired, but I won't stop until the bear is done. What will I name him? I cannot decide until he has a face.

Think of something. Make a plan. Uncle Sandor said to let him know if we needed help. He will know how to find my father. I know where the AVO headquarters are. Everybody knows. Andrassy Street 60. Bela said that's where they took our aunt and her baby. But that was a long time ago. Tears come to my eyes and I wipe them with a scrap of fabric.

I tiptoe into Bela's room. Mama is asleep on her back with her arm over her eyes. Gently I put her arm down by her side, take a blanket out of the trunk, and cover my mother.

The clock says 11:30. I should go to bed, but I am not tired and the bear is still not done. I take black thread and make him a smooth, broad nose. I choose dark glass eyes. His ears are round and stiff. When he is done, I shake off the loose threads and set him on the edge of the table. He could be Zoli. But he doesn't look like the Zoli in my class who sits so stiffly at his desk. This bear is slouching just a little. His shoulders are wide and his head is big.

I wonder who will buy him. It could be a little girl in a stroller. Or a big boy who likes to read. I look up at the bear. Then I take a piece of yellow plastic and make a nice cursive *B*. The rest of the letters are small and neat. I let the ink dry and tie the name tag to the bear with yellow ribbon. Then I carry Bela Bear to my bed.

"Kata, you will be late for school." Mama's voice is flat. "Hurry or you won't have time for breakfast."

I stand next to my mother and put my arm around her shoulders. "I know you will think of something," I say. "You always do."

"Not always." Mama is standing by the stove, stirring my cocoa.

"I can make my own breakfast," I say. "You are busy."

"Not too busy to make cocoa," Mama says. "Now get ready."

I put my school uniform on quickly and gulp down the cocoa as fast as I can. "Mama, did you see that I finished the bear?"

Mama looks over at the sewing machine. "You must have stayed up very late." Then she sees the name tag, and her eyes meet mine. "After your brother," she says softly.

"He left me," I whisper.

Mama holds me close for a minute. "Go now, Kata, or you will be late to school."

I grab my book bag and head out the door.

I'm so tired at school that I keep dozing off. In Russian class, I really fall asleep. I have no idea which verse of the poem we are on when the teacher asks me to read. He writes "1" in his grade book and goes on to the next student. "Now, everybody must remember to study for the final test," he says, looking straight at me.

During our break, I lean against the school building and close my eyes. The sun is warm on my face. "You don't look well," Anna says.

When I open my eyes, the whole playground is spinning. "I couldn't sleep last night."

"Me either." She smiles. "I kept thinking about this summer."

"What about it?" Zsuzsi asks.

Anna looks around. "Do you know Tibor?"

"Of course we know Tibor," says Zsuzsi.

"Well, we plan to meet at the swimming pool."

Zsuzsi rolls her eyes. "Little Tibi? What do you want from him?"

"I think he's cute," Anna says.

"What do you think, Kata?" Zsuzsi asks.

"Think about Tibi?" I shrug. "I don't really know him."

"But don't you think he's cute?" Anna asks.

"Sort of."

The bell rings.

We are reviewing for the final history test next week. This king and that king, this war and that war. The teacher's voice drones on. Papa is at number 60 Andrassy Street. What are they doing to him there?

"Kata."

I stand up to answer.

"Where did the sailors first revolt in 1917?"

What is she talking about? "Konigsberg," whispers Zsuzsi.

"Konigsberg," I say.

"Very good."

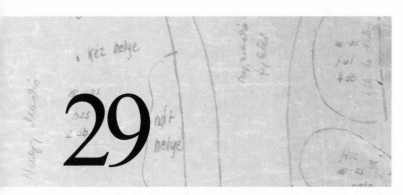

29

Mama is not at home. Of course. She said she was going to talk to Papa's supervisor. But what if the AVO came while I was at school and took my mother away too? I can cook. I can sew bears and give them to Auntie Klari to sell. With the money, I'll buy my own food.

I glance at the clock. If Mama doesn't come home in half an hour, I'll go to Uncle Sandor's apartment. I know where it is. Papa used to take me with him when he went to play chess.

I take an apple and sit down to study geography, but my eyes cannot focus on all the small maps. I'll ask Uncle Sandor to lend me enough money to buy a train ticket to Auntie Erzsi's. She will be so happy to see me. She will be surprised at how tall I am.

Only ten minutes have gone by. I turn back to the maps. The capital city of Romania is Bucharest. The doorbell rings. My brother died, I will tell the AVO. My father has been sick. Tonsillitis and ear infections. My poor father is almost deaf. Of course he will not be able to answer questions accurately, since he cannot hear. My mother is out shopping.

The bell rings again. I look through the peephole. "The mailman was just bringing the mail, so I picked yours up too," Eva says when I open the door. "Are you the only one home?"

I take a deep breath. "For now."

When I set the mail on the table, a letter catches my eye. The handwriting looks a little like Bela's, but I can't look at it closely with Eva there.

"Are you coming with me to the Pioneer meeting tomorrow?" she asks.

"I have final tests next week. I think I'd better study." I flip through the pages of the geography book.

Eva sighs. "I wish you could go instead of me."

"Why don't you quit?"

"My father would kill me. I told you, he makes me go to every single meeting, even the ones before school, so I can be a Pioneer leader next year."

"Like Comrade Toth?"

Eva nods.

"Aren't you too young?"

"My father says age is not important."

"So, what exactly do you have to do to become a leader?"

Eva looks around. "I have to go to all the meetings and write reports and stuff."

"Reports about what?"

"Like what I will do to become a good leader." Eva lowers her voice. "My father is supposed to turn in a whole list of people who have ... who don't ... who commit transgressions. And he wants me to help him."

"What is a transgression?"

"Like when people do bad things, I have to write them down."

Transgression. I say the word in my head. It sounds very serious. "Like what kind of bad things?"

Eva's voice is cracking. "That's the problem. I don't know exactly." Now I can hardly hear her words. "I really shouldn't be telling you this, but my father said that your family is one to watch."

Eva's eyes are red around the edges like she might cry. The circles around them are dark and her red pimples are bright in the sunlight. "My family?" I ask.

She nods. "My father said your father is a factory owner."

"He was," I whisper, "when I was a baby."

Eva looks at the sewing machine. "And your mother makes so many handbags and bears and everything."

"Is that a trans ... trans ..."

"Transgression."

"Transgression?"

"I don't know." Eva is crying. "I told my father that you are my best friend in the whole world."

"Did you tell him about the handbags and the bears?"

"No. But he says I have to be honest in the reports."

Our apartment is so hot I can hardly breathe. I want Eva to leave. I want to push her out the door and down the stairs along with Auntie Irene.

"I told him that nobody listens to me except you, Kata. I told him that your parents don't shout at you all the time. I told him I don't want to be a Pioneer leader, but he says I have to."

Eva leans forward. I know she wants to hug me, but I move back. I don't want her pudgy arms around my neck.

"You are the one who could be a good Pioneer leader, Kata. Comrade Toth likes you so much. The other day she thanked me for bringing you. She said that you hold more promise than anyone else in our group."

"I don't think I can go tomorrow," I say coolly.

"Please. I don't want to go by myself." Eva sniffles. She wipes her nose on her sleeve.

"Are you sure you didn't tell your father about the handbags and the bears?" I ask.

"I didn't, I promise."

"What are you going to write about our transgressions?"

Eva swallows. "If my father wants a report, he's going to have to write it himself." She stops. "But sometimes, sometimes ... I feel ... sorry for him because they're forcing him ..."

"Nobody can force anybody to write a report if they don't want to."

"Yes, they can," Eva says quickly.

"How?"

"The AVO kept him overnight," Eva whispers.

"At Andrassy Street 60?" I can hardly believe they took Eva's father.

Eva nods.

"I thought your father was the district representative of the Workers' Party."

"He is. Now. But before …" Eva is covering her face. "I don't know."

"They kept him for only one night?"

Eva looks out the window. "Now they say they made a mistake. They mixed him up. But that night, they burned him with their cigarettes," she whispers.

I suck in my breath. "And then they let him go?"

Eva nods. "They made him promise to tell on people. They'll question him again. And if he doesn't have the reports, they might … send him away."

"Away where?"

"I don't know." There are tears running down Eva's face. "But sometimes I wish he were gone so he would stop shouting at me." Eva is covering her face with her hands again and her shoulders are moving up and down. "Kata, I wish I could live in your apartment," Eva says. "Ever since I was little, I wished that … I was your sister." She takes a deep breath. "Your parents are nice and you have a brother and I don't have anyone."

I can tell Eva that my father is with the AVO right now. Maybe they are burning him with cigarettes. Maybe they are taking him someplace far away. I can tell her that Bela is gone. I can tell her that she can be like my sister for now.

But Eva might change her mind. She might write a report about my family, about the bears and handbags and my brother and everything, and give it to her father. Then the AVO will come for Mama and me too.

Eva is taking short breaths. She's trying not to cry, but sobs keep breaking through. Her shoulders are moving up and down again. I stand up and look around. Bela Bear is sitting on the sewing machine.

"Here, Eva," I say. "Here is a bear for you."

She looks up. "Your mother is making them for friends."

"This one is for you. And you know what his name is?"

She flips the tag around. Her eyes meet mine and she blushes. "Are you sure you … you don't want to keep him?"

"I'm sure. I made him."

"Yourself?"

"Pretty much."

Eva pats his golden fur and then holds him to her stomach. "He's perfect."

"Not really."

"You must miss your brother," she says.

Then we are both crying.

Eva's mother is calling. Her voice echoes in the stairwell. "I'd better go," Eva says. She holds Bela Bear toward me. "Are you sure? I mean, if you want to keep him, that's okay."

I turn away. "He's yours," I whisper.

"Thanks," she says softly. "Thanks a whole lot."

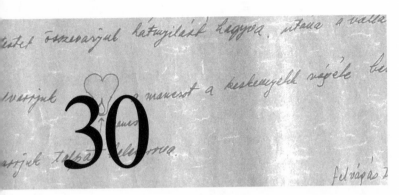

30

As soon as Eva is gone, I look at the mail. The envelope with the handwriting like Bela's is on top. It is addressed to my father, so I shouldn't open it. I take it over to the window and hold it up to the light. Could it really be from Bela? There is no return address and the postmark is smudged.

I should study, but instead I sit down at the sewing machine. There is an order for six more bears. I gave Bela Bear to Eva. How will Mama ever finish so many? I glance at the clock. Mama has been gone for over an hour. I could go to Uncle Sandor's, but what would I say? That my father is at the AVO? They are burning him with cigarettes? Eva said they kept her father overnight. Only one night. I stare out the window. Bela said they kept his friends for only a few hours. Maybe Papa is already on his way home.

I lay the wool fabric out on the floor like I've seen Mama do so often. Then I place the pattern pieces on it, careful not to waste any material. Finally I cut around the ears, down the arms, legs, and body. The head is the hardest. The three pieces are curved for the nose. It has to be just right. My scissors slip and I cut too far. Now I've wasted fabric. Mama will not be pleased. I unpin the pattern piece, move it over, and cut it again.

I start sewing the ears. I wonder what sort of bear this one will be. He could be smart like Albert, but then again maybe he's just a little bit clever. I wonder who will play with him. A three-year-old girl with curly hair and dark eyes? A girl who wanders away into the barn to find the baby goat and pet the kitten? The hay smells so sweet in the barn. She will make a home for her bear there, a cozy nest with the kitten and the mama goat and the baby one.

Mama is standing in the open doorway. I drop the bear and stand up so fast that my legs buckle. Mama shuffles over to the sofa. I pick up the bear and sit down beside her. She reaches into her pocket and takes out a folded piece of paper. It is some sort of certificate, signed by Dr. M. Laszlo. I read the small typed letters:

This is to certify that Steiner Matyas has sustained a serious hearing loss and has been unable to work for the past several weeks. He is to visit my office weekly for irrigation treatments in both ears in the hope that his hearing can be restored.

"Tomorrow I will take this to Andrassy Street," Mama says, "and I will shame them for holding a sick man."

My stomach flips. "What if they keep you there?"

"We have to try," Mama says.

"They let Eva's father go," I say.

"What?"

"Eva said the AVO took her father. They kept him overnight, and then they let him go."

"Eva's father? Really?"

I nod.

"And they let him go, just like that?"

I don't want to say the words. "First they burned him with cigarettes," I whisper.

Mama's voice is clear. "And then?"

"Then they told him to write reports against people ... people like us." My thread breaks.

"What could Eva's father say about us?" Mama asks.

"Eva told him that I am her best friend and that you are the perfect parents."

"Did you tell her anything? About Papa or Bela?"

I shake my head. "But she has seen all the bears and handbags."

"For our friends," Mama says. She is staring at the door of Bela's room. There are tears in her eyes.

"We got a letter," I say, handing Mama the envelope.

Mama gives it back to me. "You open it, Kata."

I use my needle to slit the edge. Inside is a small, folded piece of paper. My eyes move quickly over the words.

Dear Mama, Papa, Kata,

I hope this letter finds you well. I have decided to make my way to America, leaving as soon as possible.

There is an organization that is helping me get my documents in order. Please don't expect to hear from me for a while. I think it is safer for you if I don't write.

  Love,
  Bela

Mama is looking out the window.

"Read the letter," I say.

I watch Mama's eyes move slowly across the lines, stopping after each word. "America is very far," she says.

31

It is late when I finally finish the bear. I stand up and stretch. Her ears are lopsided and her head too. She is a very attentive bear, a nurse. Florence, I decide, like Florence Nightingale.

I tiptoe over to my desk with a yellow square of plastic and make a fancy *F* with a nice long tail. The next letter is smooth and tall.

"Very nice, Kata."

It is Papa. I drop the pen and it splatters ink onto the name tag.

"Now you'll have to write it over again," Papa says, hugging me so hard that I think he will never let me go.

We sit at the kitchen table. Mama makes tea even though it is the middle of the night. My eyes keep staring at Papa's neck, his cheeks, the backs of his hands. I don't see any burns. Could they have burned him under his shirt? Papa drinks his tea in big gulps.

"Slow down, Papa," Mama says. "The tea will not run away."

Papa nods. "You are right." He turns to me. "She's always right, that Mama, isn't she?" he asks.

I bury my face in my father's sweater.

Mama shows Papa the paper she got from the ear doctor.

Papa nods. "You know, I kept asking the AVO officer to repeat everything he said. 'Eh?' I kept saying." Papa starts laughing as he tells Mama and me the story. "Finally he said, 'Mr. Steiner, are you deaf?' 'Eh?' I said. He shouted in my ear, 'Mr. Steiner, are you deaf?' 'Sorry, Comrade,' I said. 'I cannot hear you.'"

"You did very well, Papa," Mama says.

"Eh?"

I want to ask Papa if they burned him with cigarettes, but he is busy reading the letter from Bela. "Why America?" Mama says finally. "Why so far away?"

"The farther the better," Papa says.

America. *Make my way to America*, Bela says. But how? In a boat? Across the whole ocean? The Danube flows into the Black Sea, but after that, I don't know where it goes. Somehow the water must go into the ocean because all the rivers flow into the sea. But which sea? Are all the oceans connected? *Don't expect to hear from me for a while.* How long is a while?

Mama and Papa sit side by side on the sofa. They are reading the letter over and over. I sit down at the sewing machine and take out the fabric for another bear.

"America is very far," Mama says finally. "Bela will be on a boat for a long time."

"Maybe he will take an airplane," Papa says.

Mama sucks in her breath. "My son on an airplane?" She shakes her head.

"I would love to sit on such a plane," Papa says.

"Me too," I say.

"If Kata and I both go, you will have to come with us," Papa says to Mama.

Mama is watching me sew. "I think you are the professional and I am the assistant," she says.

"I gave a bear to Eva," I say.

"Is it her birthday?" Mama asks.

"No. But she was sad."

"Good. I'm glad if you can help your friend."

"Kata, maybe you should go to sleep," Mama says. "And you too," she tells Papa.

"I'm not tired," Papa says.

"Were you able to sleep at Andrassy Street?"

"Not exactly." Papa is looking out the window.

"So they let you go, just like that?"

"They told me to inform on my friends and relatives."

I suck in my breath.

"But of course I couldn't hear a word they said." Papa stands up and stretches.

"What did they say about the accusations against you?"

"Nothing. Finally one officer told the other that a man as deaf as a stone can hardly be helpful."

32

Mama says I should take a nap before the Pioneer meeting. I lie down on my bed, but I can't get comfortable. Shouting is coming from downstairs. I cover my head with my blanket to keep from hearing it, but then I can hardly breathe.

I scan the titles of the books on my shelf. Bela always wanted me to read *The Count of Monte Cristo,* but I told him such a long book was boring. I take it off my shelf and open the cover. On the title page, Bela wrote, *This book is the property of Steiner Bela.* Could my brother already be on his way to America? My eyes get watery. Mama and Papa say that we will join Bela someday, but how will we cross the border? There are wire fences and guards with guns at the checkpoints. Mama says Bela will send for us once he is settled, but what can he really do? I close the book. My parents say we will go to America someday. That could mean next week or ten years from now. I wipe my face on my pillow. When we join Bela, I will bring him his book. Mama will say it is too heavy. Papa will say we can buy another copy in America. But this book will travel with me.

I reach for a slim volume that Papa once gave me called *Brush Up Your English*. I was never interested in it. I couldn't read the words, and the pictures were boring. On the first page is a picture of a boy jumping. Underneath it says, *Jack jumps*. Tomorrow I'll ask Papa to help me pronounce the words. That way when we do go to America, I'll know at least *some* English. When Bela sends for us, I will be ready.

I still cannot sleep. What if Eva's father tells the AVO that we have committed transgressions? Then we will never get to America. We will never see my brother. A lump grows in my throat.

I sit at my desk and look through the Dear Bear notebook. It seems so long ago that I made all the little drawings. I add Bela Bear to the end of the row of bear sketches. His head is bent down and his shoulders are wide. He is smiling just a little. After that I draw the girl bear, Florence.

I knock on Eva's door. "I've decided to go to the Pioneer meeting," I say.

Her eyes are swollen. "I thought you had to study."

"I'll study later."

"Okay. I'll be ready in five minutes."

I wait by the door of our building. The sun is warm but not too hot. I close my eyes and feel the heat on my face. Somebody is humming a familiar tune. A neighbor girl is sitting on the wall in the garden and humming a nursery rhyme about a cow that has no tail and no ears. Then it goes to live in a place where it gets sugar. The whole thing doesn't make any sense, but the tune is nice. The girl looks at me shyly and smiles. She is only six or seven, much too young to know about borders or transgressions. She has no idea that the AVO could come at any time and take her parents away.

When Eva emerges, we head down the hill toward the streetcar stop. I want to ask her about all the shouting, but maybe she'll be embarrassed. Maybe she's not in a talking mood. We have been on the streetcar for a few minutes when Eva says, "I told my father that I'll never be a Pioneer leader."

"What did he say?"

"He and my mother yelled at me." She swallows. "They said I'll never amount to anything."

"Do you still have to go to every meeting?"

"I guess so."

Then I ask, "What about the report?"

Eva looks down at her lap. "I told my father that I have nothing to add."

Suddenly I see where we are. "We missed the stop," I say.

Eva raises her eyes. "Who cares," she mumbles.

"We could get off at the next stop and walk back to your school."

Eva shakes her head. "Let's just skip the meeting."

"What if your parents find out?"

She shrugs.

"Your father might shout at you even more."

Eva rubs her face with her hands. "How will he know?" The streetcar is headed down toward the Danube. "How about we get off at the bridge and walk along the promenade?"

"It'll be much more fun than listening to Comrade Toth," I say. "I hate the way she takes away my pictures."

Eva looks surprised. "Really? But she likes you so much."

"I guess so," I say. "But I don't really like her."

We get off the streetcar and head down the hill. The breeze is blowing and the sun is warm. Daffodils are blooming on the corner. A boy is trying to fly a kite, but it keeps crashing into the ground. Finally his father runs with it. The kite hovers, catches the wind, and rises up over the Danube.

We head down the promenade toward the park. A girl is pulling her brother in a wagon. "Faster, faster," he says.

"I always wished I had a sister or a brother," Eva says. "But my parents said I was so much trouble, they couldn't imagine having another child."

The girl stops pulling the wagon. The boy gets out and hits her. "It's not always a lot of fun," I say, watching them fight.

"Do you and Bela fight?"

"We used to."

"Over what?"

"When we were on the farm, he said I wandered away."

"What farm?"

I tell Eva about Auntie Erzsi and the goats and how I played with the baby one in the barn. Bela was so mad when he found me there.

"Why?"

"He was always worried about everything."

"Why were you there without your parents?" Eva asks.

I tell her that we are Jewish and Auntie Erzsi agreed to keep Bela and me until the end of the war. She didn't have room to keep my parents.

"Where did they go?"

"My mother hid with somebody else. My father was taken away to a labor camp."

Eva pulls her eyebrows together. "You must have been scared without your parents."

I think for a minute. "I wasn't, really. I liked Auntie Erzsi. Bela was more scared than I was."

Eva nods. "He probably understood more about the war and everything."

I almost tell her then. I almost tell her that my brother has left forever. But I'd better not. She might change her mind about the Young Pioneers. Her father might force her to write a report. She might say something about all the bears in our apartment. Then who knows what might happen. I try to change the subject. "What are you doing this summer?"

"Nothing much. My parents are making me go to the Young Pioneers summer camp. What will you do?"

"Sew bears."

After the words are out of my mouth, I know I shouldn't have said them. Now Eva will ask if we are selling the bears, but instead she asks, "Is it fun?"

"Sort of. I like to do the faces and the name tags, but it gets tiring."

"I really like Bela Bear. He's so cute. Maybe you can teach me how to make a bear."

We go over to the swings. Eva sits and I stand with my feet on either side of her, pumping the swing. We go so high and far we are almost out over the water.

"What do you think Comrade Toth will say when she sees we are absent?" Eva shouts over the wind.

"I don't know."

"She might give us some sort of punishment."

"It might be a ... transgression."

"Maybe."

"It's worth it," I say, pumping the swing as high as I can.

33

My final tests are not too hard. I get a "5" on every one except Russian, which is a "3." I just can't remember those poems and that strange alphabet.

After the last exam, Anna and Zsuzsi and I take the streetcar to the swimming pool. There aren't many people, and the water is freezing. We put our toes in and suck in our breath. "It's like ice," Anna says.

"Okay, last one in is a rotten egg," I say, taking the plunge. Soon we are all in the water, swimming and splashing. We see Tamas from our class, and Erik. When we can't stand the cold any longer, we lie in the sun and dry off on our towels. For a minute I look up and see someone with wide shoulders and curly hair. I hold my breath. He turns our way and it's nobody I know.

"Who are you looking at?" asks Anna.

"Nobody," I say, turning my head.

I close my eyes and feel the heat of the sun on my eyelids. Where is Bela right now? In a new apartment in New York? Working at a new job? How will we know when he is ready to send for us? Will he write a letter telling us the plan?

•

Mama has finished three bears. She's never made so many in a day before. I sit next to her and start on the fourth one.

"Were your tests okay, Kata?" Mama asks.

"All except Russian."

Mama lifts her eyebrows.

"I just don't like it," I say, turning the ear of the bear right side out.

After dinner, I bring *Brush Up Your English* to the table.

"How do you say this?" I ask Papa.

He has his German book open. He is not listening to me.

"Papa."

"What is it, Kata?"

I point to the words in the book. "How do you pronounce this?"

"Jack jumps," Papa says.

"Jack jumps," I repeat.

"Is that English?" Mama asks.

"Of course it is English," Papa says.

Mama tries to repeat "Jack jumps," but it sounds like "Yuk yupsh."

Papa smiles. "Mama, are you speaking Greek?"

"This English is too difficult," Mama says, stuffing my bear's head.

I look at the bear's face. "His name is Jack," I say.

"Short and simple," Mama says. "Yack."

"Not Yack. It's J-J-Jack."

"J-J-Jack," she repeats.

"Very good," Papa says.

We go through the whole first chapter, but Mama has stopped listening. "Mama, you had better know English when we get to America," I say.

"To sew bears and handbags, Hungarian is enough," she says.

Papa is looking out the window and I see that there are tears in the corners of his eyes.

"What's wrong, Papa?" I ask.

"I miss that boy of ours," Papa says, putting his hand on mine. Then I see that where his sleeve meets his wrist, there is a small round burn.

"What if they come and get you again?" I whisper.

"Then we will think of something," he says. "As soon as we can, we will meet Bela in America."

"But how?" I ask.

"Bela will help us," he says, squeezing my hand.

In the morning, Jack is next to my bed. His bright eyes catch the sun. "Hi, Mr. Jack," I say, holding him.

Mama is at the door. "That Jack Bear is for you," she says.

"Until Aunti Klari comes to pick him up."

"No, Kata. He is really for you. For finishing the school year so well."

I can't believe it. All this time I was waiting for a bear, but now I'm not sure I want him. "But you have seven orders and now you have seven bears," I say.

"I will make another one."

I look at Mama. The lines around her eyes are deep. Klari will come soon to pick up the bear and the handbags. I don't want Mama to have to make one more bear today.

"But Mama, I've been saving scraps to make myself a bear." I show Mama my pile. "I think I have enough now if I piece them together," I say.

Mama is watching my hands smooth the bigger scraps. Then she kneels down on the floor and we decide together. "I think these two could make the body," she says softly. "And maybe we can get one arm out of this one."

Papa is reading out loud. "Jack and Jill went up the hill," he says.

"What are you talking about?" Mama asks.

"Jack and Jill went up the hill," he says again.

"Jack and Jill went up the hill," I repeat.

"Don't talk nonsense," Mama says, going back to the bear on the floor.

"Nonsense? This is English," Papa says. He finishes the poem: "Jack and Jill went up the hill to fetch a pail of water. Jack fell down and broke his crown and Jill came tumbling after."

"I don't understand," I say.

"There are two children, a brother named Jack and a sister named Jill."

"And?"

"And Jill follows her brother."

"Like me and Bela," I whisper.

"Then Jack falls down, and Jill falls down after him."

"Then they both get up," I say.

Mama and I spend a long time on the bear. Piecing the scraps together is harder than I thought. "What will you name this one?" Mama asks.

"I don't know yet," I say. "I have to wait until he is finished so I can look at his face."

"People love the bears with names," Mama says.

I show Mama my notebook with the picture of all the bears with their names.

By lunchtime, we have the pieces cut out. But Mama has handbags to make. She says that Lily and Agnes are helping, but they can't keep up with the orders. "I'll do the handles," I say.

Mama's eyes are tired. "Thank you, Kata."

After lunch, Mama asks me to run to the store to get more thread. Eva is sitting in the stairwell. Her eyes are swollen.

"What's wrong?" I ask.

"I have to go to camp soon."

"Maybe you'll like it."

"I won't," Eva says. She takes a deep breath. "I'm taking Bela," she says, bringing the bear out from under her jacket.

"I'm making a bear for myself now," I say.

"Really? Our bears can be friends. Except who knows where I'll be."

"When are you leaving?"

"Tomorrow."

"So soon?" Suddenly I know that I will miss Eva. Her parents scare me, but Eva is not like them. "Well, have a good trip. And send me a postcard."

Eva nods. I think if she talks, she will cry.

I put my arms around her shoulders. "And when you get back, we can go swimming."

When I am at the door of our building, I turn back. Eva is holding Bela Bear in front of her. One of his arms is raised. Bela is saying good-bye.

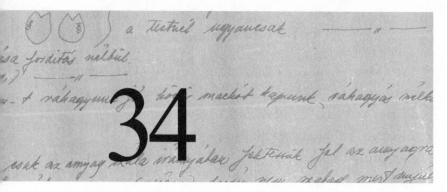

34

Mama says I am old enough to take the streetcar to the pool by myself now. But I don't really like going without Bela. I go into his room and look at the books on his shelf. *The Count of Monte Cristo* is boring. But there are others I haven't read yet, like *Oliver Twist* and *Huckleberry Finn*. If I practice a lot, maybe I will be able to read them in English.

I open *Brush Up Your English* to chapter three. "Introductions" is the name of the chapter. I start reading it out loud. "'Hello, John, how are you?' 'Fine, thank you, and you?' 'I have been feeling a little under the weather.'"

At the bottom it says that "under the weather" means not too well. "Papa," I say, pretending he is there. "Are you under the weather?"

Mama pokes her head into my room. "What are you talking about, Kata?"

"I asked Papa if he is under the weather."

"Why the weather?" she asks, looking out the window.

"'Under the weather' means you are not feeling good."

Mama shrugs. "The weather can be good or it can be bad."

"It's just an expression," I say, pointing to the line in the book.

"Those English have too many expressions," Mama says. "I can't keep them straight."

Papa comes in and we practice.

"Hello, Father, how are you?"

"Just fine. How about you?"

"A little under the weather."

"Are you ill?"

"I have a ... headache," I say, looking at the list of ailments at the bottom of the page.

"I have a stomach ache," Papa says.

"I have a broken leg," I read.

"I have appendicitis," Papa says.

"I have a fever," I say.

"With so many ailments, how can we go to America?" Mama asks, smiling.

"So you do understand some English," I say.

"Very little."

"More than you think," Papa says.

"When will we leave?" I ask.

"After Bela has a place to live and a job, we will start making our plans," Mama says.

"But I thought the borders were impossible to cross."

"Difficult, yes. But nothing is impossible," Papa says.

"What will we do to earn money in America?"

"You worry too much, Kata. We'll think of something," Mama says.

"We can sew handbags and bears," I say.

Mama nods. "I imagine that American children like bears as much as Hungarian children do."

"And American machines also need gears," Papa says. He follows Mama into the kitchen to set the table.

When Mama calls me for lunch, I say in English, "I'll be right there."

"What?"

"The noodles smell good," I say, breathing deeply.

"Then come and eat," Mama says, smiling.